# 'I still haven't lea[...]
# wanting you.'

'Sander...' Shattered by that admission of continuing desire from the husband she was in the midst of divorcing, Tally stared at him, her emotions in turmoil to the extent that she no longer knew what she was thinking or feeling.

'In fact, wanting you is driving me absolutely crazy, *yineka mou*,' Sander admitted darkly.

And for the first time in longer than Tally could remember her body leapt with actual physical hunger. Was it the dark-chocolate luxury of his deep voice which provoked the sudden rise of those long-buried needs? Or the sinfully sexual charge of his golden eyes? Tally had no idea, but she felt a sudden clenching tight sensation low in her pelvis, while her nipples were stung into tight swollen buds. Her mouth ran dry.

Like a rabbit caught in car headlights, Tally gazed back at Sander, feeling as vulnerable as if he had stripped her naked and marched her out into a busy street. *Yineka mou*—my wife, he'd called her. And she *was* still his wife, she reminded herself helplessly…

# THE VOLAKIS VOW

*A marriage made of secrets…*

An enthralling two-part story by bestselling author
Lynne Graham

Book One:
## THE MARRIAGE BETRAYAL

Tally Spencer, an ordinary girl with no experience of
relationships… Sander Volakis, an impossibly rich and
handsome Greek entrepreneur… Their worlds collide
in an explosion of attraction and passion. Sander's
expecting to love her and leave her, but for Tally this is
love at first sight. Both are about to find that it's not easy
to walk away…*because Tally is expecting Sander's baby
and he is being blackmailed into making her his wife!*

**THE MARRIAGE BETRAYAL
is still available to read via www.millsandbook.co.uk**

Book Two:
## BRIDE FOR REAL

Just when they thought their hasty marriage was
finished, Tally and Sander are drawn back together and
the passion between them is just as strong… But Sander
has hidden reasons for wanting his wife in his bed again,
and Tally also has secrets…*and neither is prepared for
what this tempestuous reunion will bring…*

Can you wait to find out what happens?

# BRIDE FOR REAL

BY
LYNNE GRAHAM

MILLS & BOON

First published in Great Britain 2011
by Mills & Boon, an imprint of Harlequin (UK) Limited,
Eton House, 18-24 Paradise Road, Richmond, Surrey TW9 1SR

© Lynne Graham 2011

ISBN: 978 0 263 88676 4

Harlequin (UK) policy is to use papers that are natural, renewable
and recyclable products and made from wood grown in sustainable
forests. The logging and manufacturing process conform to the
legal environmental regulations of the country of origin.

Printed and bound in Spain
by Blackprint CPI, Barcelona

# BRIDE FOR REAL

# PROLOGUE

BRILLIANT dark eyes grim, Sander studied the photo of his wife, small and sexy in a scarlet evening gown and wrapped in another man's arms.

He was disturbed to appreciate that he was in shock. The white heat of the rage that followed made him light-headed and scoured him inside like a cleansing flame, leaving him feeling curiously hollow. Robert Miller, well, that wasn't a surprise, was it? Sander had noted at the Westgrave Manor party two years earlier that Miller had wanted Tally the minute he'd laid eyes on her. Just as Sander had, once. But in spite of his simmering fury, Sander pushed the newspaper away with a careless hand and glanced at his watching father to say lightly like a practised card player hiding his hand, *'So?'*

'When will you be fully free of her?' Petros Volakis demanded sourly, as if an estranged wife, whose new single life was being fully documented by the media, was an embarrassment to the family name.

'I'm free now,' Sander pointed out with a shrug, for although divorce proceedings still had a way to go, an official separation was already in place.

As his attention roamed involuntarily back to the

newspaper lying close by he questioned the strength of his reaction to seeing Tally with someone else. They were getting a divorce. It should be no surprise that she was back on the social circuit. But, like a man forced to stand still while hot pitch was slowly dripped onto his skin, Sander was in torment. Why? Prior to their break-up Tally had brandished her indifference to Sander like a banner and he had assumed that no man could breach her barriers. The idea that another man might have succeeded where he had failed outraged and challenged him. 'I don't see you featuring in the gossip columns the way you did before you married,' the older man remarked with more insight than Sander usually ascribed to him.

'I've grown up,' Sander countered drily. 'I'm also more discreet.'

'*She* was a mistake but we'll say no more about it,' Petros commented, noting the hardening of his son's stubborn jaw line with a wary eye.

His lean, darkly handsome face uninformative, Sander *had* nothing to say, at least nothing worth saying. He marvelled that his parents, who had not even offered him sympathy on the death of his firstborn son, could think that any aspect of his marriage could be their business. But then, relations had long been chilly between Sander and his mother and father. His elder brother, Titos, the family favourite, had died in a tragic accident and, although it was only thanks to Sander that Volakis Shipping had since recovered from his brother's disastrous management, Sander was still being made to feel a very poor second-best in the son stakes. And now, all of a sudden, he was disturbingly conscious that his meteoric triumphs in business were in stark contrast to a frankly abysmal rating in his private life

Tally, in contrast, had moved on from their marriage at startling speed and was evidently enjoying considerable success: new business, new home, *new man*. That knowledge infuriated Sander, who remembered a much more innocent Tally, a glowing girl who had once been too excited to breathe when he'd kissed her. He could not stand to think of her in bed with Robert Miller, and the awareness shocked him because he had never seen himself as a possessive man…

# CHAPTER ONE

'WHEN will your divorce from Volakis be final?' Robert Miller asked casually.

Suspecting that his question was anything but casual, Tally stiffened. Her bright green eyes wary, she averted her head, light glancing over the smooth coil of hair at the nape of her neck and picking out its natural streaks of brighter orange as she leafed through a fabric sample book. 'In a couple of months…'

'It feels like it's been going on for ever,' Robert complained, his impatience with the situation unconcealed. 'I'm getting tired of the fact that everyone assumes we're only friends—'

'We *are* friends and you're my business partner,' Tally responded lightly, knowing that he wanted more but not at all sure, even yet, that she would ever be able to give it to him.

It was only a year since Sander, the loss of their child and the sad debris of their failed marriage had broken Tally's heart into tiny shattered pieces. The last thing she wanted in her life was the stress of a man with expectations she couldn't fulfil. It was fun to meet Robert for casual dinner dates and occasionally accompany him to more formal events but she wasn't ready for a full-on relationship at present. She valued his friendship and his business guidance and support, but she had yet to feel any desire to take matters to a more intimate level. Sander, she reflected painfully, seemed to have killed those feelings stone dead.

Yet at six feet tall with dark hair and bright blue eyes, Robert was a very attractive man and a successful software designer with his own company. Nine months earlier, Robert had given Tally her first major project when he'd engaged her to make over the interior of his London Docklands apartment. Thanks to the publicity garnered by that job, Tally's brand new interiors firm had expanded rapidly to cope with a steady influx of keen clients. Although business was good, Tally had still found it impossible in the depressed economic climate to get a bank to invest in the future of Tallulah Design. Times were hard for newly self-employed people and when Robert offered her the finance she'd needed to set up her office in upmarket premises and hire extra staff, she had been very grateful. For the past six months Robert had acted as a supportive silent partner.

Sadly, an unpleasant surprise was in store for Tally that afternoon when her assistant, Belle, told her she had a confidential call on hold for her. 'I've been advised that the house you shared with Mr Volakis in France is about to be sold,' her solicitor told her. 'I've also been informed that if you want anything from the house you will need to go there and collect it.'

Thoroughly taken aback by that news, Tally grimaced and thanked the older man for passing on the information. She tried not to think about the house she had loved being sold, but it was no use; she had stamped her personality and style on the rambling property and she had once been very happy there. Knowing that it would soon belong to someone else filled her with a tide of regret. She had not been prepared for Sander to sell the house, though she could not have explained why. Would it have been a comfort to picture him there with some other woman? Absolutely not. Indeed she shivered at that offensive image and hurriedly suppressed it. When so many more important things had been lost, it would be ridiculous to bemoan the loss of bricks and mortar and memories of more contented times.

Even so, divorcing Sander was proving to be an ongoing challenge, Tally conceded ruefully as she checked her diary to work out if she could make a trip to France that very weekend and get the matter over and done with. Their divorce could certainly not be labelled a civilised break-up. Had Sander so desired, he could easily have had her belongings shipped back to the UK for her to sort out; but he had made not one single helpful gesture since their separation. He had not seen her; in fact he had, at one point, flatly refused to speak to her and had cut her out as though she had never been a part of his life.

Was that because *she* had walked out on *him*? Get over it, Sander, Tally thought angrily. If anything, she was proud of the fact that she'd had the courage to break free of a marriage that was making both of them unhappy. Since then she had read that, statistically speaking, marriages very rarely survived the death of a child.

Driving home to her apartment, Tally had to blink back a hot surge of tears and suppress the distressing recollections threatening to tear her apart. She had got over the worst of the anger, the self-pity and the bitterness; but, without warning, grief could still roll in over her like a suffocating blanket and it would be hours until she could function normally again.

Sander, however, had not suffered from that problem. Grief had not immobilised Sander in any way. During the wretched months when Tally's life had fallen apart and she had sunk into depression, Sander had contrived to rebuild Volakis Shipping into a lean, mean, fighting machine of a booming business and had won lucrative new transportation contracts with Asian factories. At a conservative estimate Sander had quadrupled his financial worth during that contentious period of their lives. Yet Tally, determined to stand on her own financial feet as her mother had never contrived to do, had refused to accept a penny from her husband once they had parted.

Tally had not felt entitled to benefit from her estranged husband's wealth. After all, Sander had only married her at her father's instigation because she'd been pregnant. That brutal truth had come back to haunt her once their marriage was in crisis. In a relationship that lacked a sound foundation she had decided that it was unrealistic to hope that time would cure the tensions between them. Indeed she had had to stop and ask herself why she was still struggling to hold onto a man who had never returned her feelings. And that, in a nutshell, was why she believed their marriage had broken down:

he had never loved her. She was also utterly convinced that Sander must have been relieved to get his freedom back.

'Are you getting a share of the house in France?' her mother, Crystal, demanded that evening on the phone when Tally mentioned her plans for the weekend. For more than a year Tally had seen little of her mother because Crystal was engaged to Roger, a retired British businessman, and had made her home in Monaco with him.

'You know I don't need Sander's money—'

'I think you're being very short-sighted. I *always* needed your father's money and don't know how I'd have managed without it!' Crystal asserted, referring to the Greek businessman, Anatole Karydas, who had supported Crystal and Tally, his illegitimate daughter, right up until Tally completed her education.

'I'm managing fine just now,' Tally retorted.

'But be sensible and think of the future. Take a van over with you and empty the place!' Crystal advised without hesitation. 'By all accounts, Sander Volakis is as rich as sin and he's not going to miss a few sticks of furniture. You walked out on a *very* wealthy man!'

Aware that Crystal genuinely believed that a woman should hang on for grim death to any rich man for the sake of her long-term security, Tally, who was far more independent, had the tact to swallow back an acerbic retort. She might not see eye to eye with her parent on many subjects but she was very attached to the older woman. Nonetheless, it was Binkie—Mrs Binkiewicz, a Polish widow—who had virtually brought Tally up.

It was then Binkie whom Tally missed the most when life was tough. Binkie had acted as Tally and Sander's housekeeper in the South of France; and when their marriage had ended the older woman had returned to the UK and had taken a job with a family in Devon.

That Friday afternoon, Tally flew into Perpignan airport. Soon after she arrived she received a surprising phone call from her mother. Crystal, who had been living in Monaco with Roger for the past eighteen months, announced without the smallest preamble that she would be returning to London the next day.

'My goodness, that's very sudden. Has something happened between you and Roger?' Tally enquired gingerly, conscious that her mother's love life tended to be rather unsettled.

'Roger and I have decided to call it a day.' Crystal's tone was defensive and Tally wisely made no comment. 'I assume I can stay with you until I've got somewhere of my own sorted out...'

'Of course you can!' Tally exclaimed. 'Are you all right?'

'Nothing lasts for ever,' her mother said flatly and that was the end of the call; Crystal evidently being in no mood to talk.

A slim figure in a purple print sundress, Tally collected a hire car to drive into the foothills of the Pyrenees. The old farmhouse, reached by a narrow private road that snaked through tortuous bends up a steep hill, rejoiced in glorious views. With extensive wooded grounds that were in turn surrounded by a working vineyard and orchards, it also enjoyed great privacy. Tally was very tense as she parked outside the stone house with its vine-covered, wrought-iron loggia. Her solicitor had assured her that he would inform Sander's representative so that she could gain access to the property. But still not knowing what form that access would take, she first knocked on the door. Only when there was no response did she dig out the key she had never returned and made use of it.

The evocative scent of lavender and beeswax flared her nostrils in the terracotta-tiled hall and she was surprised to see a beautiful arrangement of flowers adorning a side table. There were no fallen petals either. Presumably the house was being as well maintained as though it were still occupied to make it appear more appealing to buyers. Even so it was distinctly eerie to walk back into the marital home she had abandoned over a year earlier and pick up on a familiar ambience that hinted that she might only have walked away the day before.

There were more flowers in the airy main reception room and a pile of the most recent interior design publications lying on the coffee table. Pale drapes were ruffling in the fresh air filtering through an open window. She spotted a small sculpture she and Sander had bought together in Perpignan and her heart lurched, for she remembered that day so clearly. Then, happily pregnant, ignorant of the tragedy to come, she had nagged Sander into taking some rare time off and spending the day with her. They had laughed and talked at length over a leisurely lunch before wandering into the art gallery and spotting the sensually curved stone figure of a couple.

Emerging from her reverie with hot cheeks, Tally realised that she was almost mesmerised by the atmosphere that so strongly evoked the past. She shook her head as though to clear it. Would she really want to take that sculpture and its attendant memories back to London with her? She thought not and mounted the oak stairs to the upper floor. Her heart started beating very fast when she entered the main bedroom. She could remember what a state she had left things in there, with clothes scattered around as she hastily packed only what she could conveniently carry in one case. Now she peered into a wardrobe in the dressing room and saw the same items all neatly hung up, the drawers full of immaculately folded garments.

Emerging from the room in a dazed state, she fell still outside a door at the end of the landing and lost colour. She had to breathe in deep, perspiration breaking out on her brow, before she could make herself depress the handle to push the door wide open. She froze on the threshold in surprise—the enchanting nursery that she had furnished with such love and hope for the future no longer existed. Her shaken eyes scanned the freshly painted walls and full-sized bedroom furniture. There was nothing now to remind her of what had once been; but the memories inside her own head, she acknowledged. She was surprised but relieved that the baby equipment, colourful wallpaper and toys were gone. In the months after the stillbirth of her little boy, Tally had haunted that room, pointlessly, painfully dreaming of what might have been.

The dulled repetitive clack of rotor blades in the

distance sent Tally to the landing window where she focused on a black helicopter moving in the cloudless blue sky over the valley. Sander had taken to flying in and out during the last months they had spent in France, citing the advantage of his being able to work while someone else transported him. By then it had sunk in on her that she was married to an unashamed workaholic to whom time meant money and the eternal pursuit of profit. A pregnant wife and a marriage needing attention had been at the very foot of Sander's to-do list. Of course it would not be Sander coming to visit today, Tally reflected wryly, moving away to pull open a storage cupboard where cases were mercifully still stored.

She would make a start by packing her clothes and then check out the rest of the house for anything she felt she could not live without. Sheets that smelled of Sander, she thought straight away before she could suppress that inappropriate notion. In fact where on earth had that ridiculous thought come from? It was the crazy spell cast by this stupid house getting into her brain and confusing her, she decided angrily. It had been a very long time since such an idea had come naturally to her.

Tally was piling clothing into a case and paying scant attention to the rules of good packing when the noise of the helicopter apparently landing nearby drew her back to the window with a frown of curiosity. By then, the craft had landed on the pad at the edge of the orchard and through the screening mass of summer shrubbery in the grounds she recognised the colourful red 'V' logo on its side: V for Volakis. Her heart started beating very fast. It couldn't be Sander, it couldn't *possibly* be Sander!

As Tally backed away unconsciously from the glass she saw a tall, black-haired man in a business suit striding towards the house and shock almost stopped her heart beating altogether. The leashed masculine power of Sander's proud carriage and long stride were unmistakeable. Something shamefully akin to panic assailed Tally and, for a split second, she seriously thought of stepping into the storage cupboard where she had found the cases and closing the door. She soon shook off that nonsensical idea but she was still frozen on the landing when she heard the front door open.

'Tally—where are you? It's Sander,' a painfully familiar accented drawl announced; and fingered down the length of her spine like a mocking caress.

Her grip on the banister tightened and she moved stiffly to the head of the stairs before starting reluctantly down them, a slender very straight-backed small figure sporting an unconvincing smile. 'I've been packing. What on earth are you doing here?'

'This is still my house,' Sander reminded her softly.

Black-haired head tipped back at an almost aggressive angle, he subjected his estranged wife to an intent scrutiny because it felt like a lifetime since he had last seen her. He instantly noted the changes in her and disliked them. Her curls were gone, replaced by a sleek coil of straightened hair worn in a classic style that made her look older; and her summer dress was formal enough to have met even his mother's strict standards of ladylike grooming. As always, though, Tally's make-up was subtle, highlighting the undeniable appeal of her big green eyes and soft, full, pink mouth and the freckles scattered across her nose. His chest felt strangely tight. He could only think that he had liked that tousled torrent of rebellious curls and her once youthfully chaotic sense of fashion. Perhaps he just didn't like people to change, he told himself, uneasy with the strength of his reaction

'You must've planned this! I don't believe your arrival while I'm here could be a coincidence,' Tally condemned, struggling not to notice just how incredibly handsome he still was or how wonderfully his thick sooty lashes enhanced his lustrous dark eyes. He was clean-shaven, immaculate in a navy designer suit of faultless cut, and she couldn't drag her mesmerised gaze from him. The edge of panic inside her snapped taut like a nerve end pulling, goose bumps of awareness rising on the exposed skin of her arms.

She hated Lysander Volakis for the pain and disillusionment he had put her through. She had loved him once—loved him far too much for comfort or relaxation. But a few weeks after their wedding when she had discovered that he had been virtually blackmailed into marrying her because she'd been pregnant, she had attempted to let him go free again. She had walked out then but instead of letting her go he had followed her to the airport and persuaded her that he felt enough for her to give their marriage another chance. She still despised herself for being weak enough to give him that chance. She had dragged out her own suffering because, for a few brief months while on his very best behaviour, he had made her exceedingly happy. Then, when she was at the very height of her rose-coloured expectations of their marriage and looking forward to motherhood, she had lost everything and he had not been there for her; he had not been there for her at all. She had travelled from the warmth of sunlight into the cold of winter.

'I've never believed in coincidences,' Sander fielded with more than a hint of provocation that dragged her thoughts right back to the present. 'Naturally I knew you would be here. We can divide up the contents together.'

Having stiffened at that almost teasing intonation, Tally gritted her teeth. 'I don't think that's a good idea.'

'Wouldn't Robert like it?' Sander quipped, brilliant eyes like bright chips of golden challenge in his lean strong face.

'I don't know what you're talking about,' Tally responded flatly, uneasily aware of the sparks smouldering in the atmosphere and the essentially volatile nature of Sander's temperament.

Yet she saw changes in Sander too. His recent dazzling success in the business world had boosted the element of darkness in him, giving his lean, strong features a tougher, more ruthless edge and accentuating his hard masculinity. Sander had also acquired an intimidating degree of implacability. And she noted now, registering in surprise, that in the aftermath of their marriage her estranged husband also believed that he had an axe to grind and was in no mood to let bygones be bygones. At that moment it struck her as strange that she had never before acknowledged the likelihood that he might blame her for things just as she blamed him. In retrospect, she was shaken by the extent of her tunnel vision and her view of herself as the victim of his cruel insensitivity. Had she truly fallen into the trap of believing that she was a perfect wife?

'Miller wouldn't like the fact that you're here in this house alone with me,' Sander proclaimed in a deceptively indolent tone.

Tally was tempted to say that Robert Miller minded his own business but that would immediately reveal that theirs was a friendly rather than intimate relationship and she did not see why she should hand Sander that interesting information on a plate. No doubt he would be amused to learn that when she had last made love with a man it had been him; and that had been at least eighteen months ago. She knew Sander's hot-blooded nature and was certain that he would have moved on much sooner than she had contrived to do. A bitterness she could not suppress rose like bile in her tight throat as she still could not bear to think of Sander with anyone else.

'Robert knows better than to try and tell me what to do,' Tally replied drily, her chin lifting, green eyes glinting as if to say: Stick that in your pipe and smoke it.

Sander released a husky laugh that purred down her backbone like a taunting scratch. 'You surprise me; you liked it when *I* did it…'

And that crack smashed through Tally's superficial

shell of civility like a brick and made her fingers flex like claws and her face burn as red and hot with mortification as any fire. She knew exactly what he was getting at. In the early months of their relationship, Sander had often told her what to do in bed while he explained what he enjoyed. Not only had she had no objection to that intimate education, but she'd also discovered that it turned her on.

'That's it…I'm leaving!' Tally snapped furiously, stepping past him to snatch at the car keys she had tossed down on the side table. 'You can dump my stuff. I don't want any of it!'

But Sander's reflexes were much faster than hers and long brown fingers scooped up the keys a split second before she could. 'You're not driving off in the temper you're in—'

'Give me those keys!' Tally launched at him in a burning rage at his interference.

'How long did you wait before you welcomed Miller into your bed?' Sander enquired, relishing the sight of her all shaken up, stray strands of hair flying loose from the smooth bun at the nape of her neck while her green eyes crackled like fireworks. All of a sudden she was the woman he remembered again. No other woman of his acquaintance had ever equalled her passion, but the conviction that she had taken another man as a lover was like a knife in his chest and he couldn't leave the subject alone.

'You've got no right to ask me that!' Tally hurled, her cheeks burning as she reached for the keys.

Much taller than she was, Sander simply held the keys

out of her reach. 'I'm still your husband and naturally
I'm curious—you barred me from your bed for months
before we broke up,' he reminded her harshly, his hard
jaw line grim.

'We're almost divorced. I'm not having this conversation with you—now give me those keys!' Tally hissed
back at him in vexation.

'No,' Sander responded in Greek. 'I won't enable you
to get behind the wheel in a blind rage…'

'Oh, so caring all of a sudden!' Tally raked back at
him in a furious hiss of condemnation that she could
not restrain. 'Where did that caring guy go when we
lost our child?'

Sander froze as though she had struck him. His dark
eyes blazed with hostility before he veiled them, and
his superb cheekbones clenched into hard angular lines
below his bronzed skin. 'That's not something I'm willing to discuss—'

'No, I didn't think it would be,' Tally spat back with
raw contempt. 'Not with your track record for working
eighteen-hour days, or being back at your desk the day
after the funeral of our child. All you care about is
making more money…it doesn't matter that in comparison to most people you are already rich as Croesus, you
never seem to have enough money to be satisfied!'

Thick black lashes lifted on blistering, dark golden
eyes as direct as knives aimed at a target. 'How *dare*
you? You carried our son, so you're the only one allowed
to be sensitive and have feelings, is that right?'

Unprepared for the immediacy of that scorching
comeback, Tally muttered, 'Well, er…'

'We all cope with grief in different ways. I could have got drunk and slept with other women to express *my* wounded feelings,' he grated in a tone of derision. 'But that's not who I am. I'm not into therapy or wallowing in emotion either, wasn't brought up that way...sorry. In my family we don't whinge or talk about stuff like that. I worked every goddamned hour I could because the same day that I lost my son I lost my wife as well and working was the only way I could handle it!'

Totally disconcerted by that explosive response, which roared from him like a tornado set suddenly free from a cage, Tally had fallen back several steps in shock. She was already regretting her attack on him, wincing at how unwise it had been to break open the wound of that painful subject when she was still in the process of healing. Now catching the sheer rawness in his voice, and the caustic charge of bitter reproach in his hard gaze, Tally was paralysed to the spot and recognising in Sander a depth of emotion she had not acknowledged he might possess. Her conscience was already censuring her ill-considered words. Now she was asking herself why she had so hugely underestimated what he might be feeling when their child was born dead.

'What do you mean...you lost your wife?' Tally prompted unevenly, reluctant to ask but unable to let the statement stand unchallenged.

'You acted as if you had cornered the market on grief and you turned into a zombie. You wouldn't talk to me or go out or do anything but cry. You were suffering from depression but when I tried to persuade you to see a doctor or even a counsellor you went bonkers and told me that I couldn't possibly understand what you were going through!'

'I didn't think you did...I was all screwed up inside myself.' Tally struggled to defend her past behaviour, her heart beating so fast with tension that she could hardly breathe.

But Sander was not yet finished. Seeing her back inside the house where everything had so suddenly fallen apart had brought the past alive again for him in a way he had not foreseen. He was also reacting in a way he had not known he might and it was one of the very few times in his life that he was not fully in control. He had tried to swallow back the furious words that had come out of nowhere at him but found that he could not silence them, for his sense of injustice still burned deep and strong. 'When I suggested we have another baby you reacted like that was unforgivable and you screamed that you didn't want another child!' Sander bit out in wrathful reminder. 'And when I made the very great mistake of trying to get back into bed with you again you behaved as if it was an attempted rape!'

To say that Tally regretted what she had invited with her emotional attack on him would have been a severe understatement. Pale as milk, she was trembling with perturbation and disbelief, reeling in dismay from the bitter accusing anger he could not conceal. One minute she had been fighting him for her car keys, the *next*...?

'I'm sorry,' she framed shakily, appalled that she had surrendered entirely to her own pain after their loss while flatly refusing to recognise that he was having a tough time as well.

Sander loosed a harsh laugh. 'Sorry's not enough, is it? Sorry doesn't fix anything!' he flung back at her without hesitation. 'Our baby dying didn't stop me wanting you, it made me need you more…'

Shame filled Tally in the instant that she recognised that they had let each other down. Neither of them had been capable of keeping their relationship alive in the maelstrom of grief and misunderstanding that had followed the arrival of their stillborn son.

Sander tossed the keys back down on the table and turned his darkly handsome head back to her, eyes as black as pitch in the sunlight and glinting with emotions she couldn't read. 'And I still haven't learned how to *stop* wanting you,' he breathed in a sizzling undertone that stung her like a hot jet of steam on tender skin. 'Is there some magical combination of aversion responses that I lack? You did a hell of a number on my libido, Tally!'

'Sander…' Shattered by that admission of continuing desire from the husband she was in the midst of divorcing, Tally stared at him. Her emotions in turmoil to the extent that she no longer knew what she was thinking or feeling.

'In fact, wanting you is driving me absolutely crazy, *yineka mou*,' Sander admitted darkly.

And for the first time in longer than Tally could remember, her body leapt with actual physical hunger. She was astonished as she had felt nothing for so long that she had believed that that side of her nature might be gone for ever. Was it the dark chocolate luxury of his deep voice that provoked the sudden rise of those long-buried needs? Or the sinfully sexual charge of his dark golden eyes? Tally had no idea but she felt a sudden clenching tight sensation low in her pelvis while her nipples stung into tight swollen buds of desire. Her mouth ran dry.

Like a rabbit caught in car headlights in the dark Tally gazed back at Sander, feeling as vulnerable as if he had stripped her naked and marched her out into a busy street. *Yineka mou*, my wife, he'd called her. And she *was* still his wife, she reminded herself helplessly.

'Any idea what I can do about it?' Sander husked that question, strolling closer with the silent elegant grace that was as much a part of him as his physical strength.

'No, no idea at all.' Tally had gone rigid, suddenly aware of a danger that she had not realised she might face. She had married a manipulative man and she knew it; indeed, she had once gloried in the level of intelligence and cunning that generally kept him several steps ahead of his business competitors. Sander was a remarkably clever and shrewd guy and now, *somehow*, she had no idea how, he was pushing her buttons and making her feel things she did not want to feel. As he advanced she backed away until she was trapped between him and the door.

'You push me much too close to the edge, *yineka mou*,' Sander murmured, tilting down his darkly handsome head and running the angular side of his jaw back and forth over the smooth soft line of her cheek like a jungle cat nuzzling for attention. The familiar sandalwood and jasmine scent of his expensive after-shave lotion made her nostrils flare while the faint rasp of his rougher skin scored her nerve endings into life.

Suddenly Tally felt like someone pinned to a cliff edge, in danger and swaying far too close to a treacherous drop. She didn't want to be there, she didn't want to fall either, but any concept of choice was wrested from her when Sander found her mouth and kissed her, strong hands firm on her slim shoulders to hold her still...

# CHAPTER TWO

THAT single kiss was like dying and being reborn in the heady space of a moment. For one minute Tally was full of doubt and antagonism and the next she was seduced by the instant flow of response and the emotional intensity of her mood.

Her skin was cold and clammy with shock but her mouth was on fire beneath his, her nerve endings tingling as he pried her lips apart and plunged his tongue into the tender interior of her mouth. It was passion at its most primal level and a startled sound of protest broke in her throat as the naked flood of chemical reaction smashed down her barriers. Her head swam, her legs trembled violently and her hands clutched at his suit jacket to steady herself. His breath mingled with hers, sweet, *so* sweet, it was an unbearable aphrodisiac and her fingers rose to spear into his thick black hair and hold him to her while trading kiss for passionate kiss and revelling in the pressure of his warm sensual mouth on hers.

The breadth of his muscular chest crushed the swollen contours of her breasts and she pushed against him, defenceless in the grip of her overriding need to get even closer to him. A big hand spread across her buttocks and urged her into more intimate contact and she rocked against him, thrilled by the long hard ridge of his arousal, which even clothing could not conceal. Her hand slid down between them, small but highly effective fingers drawn into tracing the thrusting power of his masculinity. With a guttural groan he shifted even closer, inviting her touch while he bent down and used his own hands to lift her dress. His long sure fingers trailing up over the exposed length of her thighs until she shivered and shook with longing.

The heat at the heart of her was more than she could withstand and her thighs pressed together tightly as if to seal in the ache of need before easing apart again. She shivered as he found her most sensitive spot with skilled insistence, for her body was on a hair-trigger high after so many months of abstinence. He rubbed the tiny bud and she moaned out loud, quivering in his hold like an eager racehorse at the starting line—out of breath and empty of thought, fully possessed by her hunger. She felt the delicate band of fabric round her hips tighten and then it tore as, with a sound of impatience, Sander ripped her knickers in two to gain access to the damp pink folds so ready for his attention.

A choked cry escaped her as he explored the swollen silky flesh between her thighs and then he dropped down to his knees and used his mouth and his tongue on the tender tissue. Beneath that sensual onslaught Tally's legs shook like mad. It was his arms that held her steady when all control was wrested from her by her enthralled response to his exquisite carnal expertise. Her body was on the very edge, surging and hurtling towards orgasm, when he sprang upright and lifted her. Something made of china broke noisily and he brought her bottom down on a cool surface but neither of those bewildering facts could interfere with the fire raging out of control inside her.

Sander hauled her back to the edge of the table with impatient hands and parted her thighs. He slid into her, long and impossibly thick and hard, stretching her honeyed channel to capacity. As he withdrew and then slammed back into her swollen softness again the delirious excitement washed back in an intoxicating tide. With each bold stroke erotic ripples of pleasure assailed her and he held her to him, his hands firm on her hips as he thrust deeper into her with every rhythmic movement. She was out of control and out of her mind with excitement. When he drove her into a climax she screamed in release, shuddering and shaking from the seething intensity of sensation that threatened to tear her body apart as she travelled from the height of stressed-out tension to ecstatic limpness.

'You are still the most incredibly sexy woman I've ever met,' Sander growled, breathing audibly as he pressed a string of appreciative kisses across the bridge of her nose.

Closing strong arms round her, Sander lifted her off the table to carry her upstairs. She was only dimly conscious of the fact that he was crunching over the broken shards of pottery and scattered blooms that were all that now remained of the floral arrangement that had sat on the table until they'd sent it flying.

So stunned by what had happened between them that she couldn't think straight, Tally was nonetheless struggling to regain control. 'What are you doing?' was the best she could manage.

Sander did not respond. Dark golden eyes vibrant, he scanned her flushed face and simply settled her down on what had once been the marital bed. But then he had no desire to talk about anything other than the most superficial things. He had too many recollections of attempts to talk that had blown up in his face over a year earlier. Now, playing safe in silence, he wrenched back the bed linen, ignoring it when the silken bedspread spilled down in a heap on the oak floor. He followed Tally down to the mattress and began to kiss her again with a hunger that had not abated in the slightest.

Sander had always been great at kissing. The ravishing sensual force of his mouth on hers again rocked her from inside out. Nothing and nobody tasted quite as good as Sander. Roused from satiated weakness, she revelled in the renewed response of her own body, stretching up to kiss him back eagerly while he shed his clothing in fits and starts. The level of his continuing desire enthralled her and made her suspect that perhaps her estranged husband had been more faithful to her memory than she had ever had reason to hope. Surely only self-denial could make him want her so badly?

Tally was desperate to touch him, her palms skimming across his broad satin-smooth shoulders and down over his muscular, hair-roughened pectoral muscles before moving more skittishly lower.

'Don't tease me, *yineka mou*,' Sander growled in a

roughened undertone, his flat stomach muscles contracting beneath her spread fingers while a tremor of anticipation shook his long lean body against hers in a way that made her feel incredibly desirable.

'I won't…' Tally collided with hot golden eyes and felt her heart jump. As he shifted against her, inviting her touch with the raw sexuality that only grief had made her resist, she refused to think of anything but the moment.

In the back of her mind Tally knew and accepted that later their encounter would demand a strict accounting from her and just then she was painfully aware that she couldn't face it. How could she confront the conflict and mess of responses that Sander had roused in her from the moment she had walked out of his life and match it with her loss of control over events that afternoon? But, even as she avoided examining what she was doing, she was taking strong note of the fact that the guy she had let go to reclaim his freedom was getting straight back into bed with her the first chance he got. That gave her the most colossal kick of satisfaction and pleasure. It encouraged her to entertain the stunning idea that there might not have been other women in his life since their separation. And that heady suspicion somehow made everything that had occurred feel acceptable to her.

'You're irresistible, *yineka mou*, ' Sander purred, cupping a pouting breast and catching the swollen pink peak between thumb and finger so that she quivered, heat rising from the very heart of her in response. 'I can't get enough of you.'

He wanted her again, wanted her even more fiercely

than the first time, the pulse at his groin more pressing than he could bear. He crushed her reddened mouth under his again and her senses drowned in the intoxicating flood of almost painful arousal thrumming through her reawakened body. Muttering her name against her lips, he pulled her to him and turned her over, groaning his acute pleasure against her cheek as he sank his bold shaft into her lush clinging warmth all over again. And if wildness had distinguished their first bout of intimacy, control and steady intensity distinguished the second. As he held her fast and plunged into her velvety depths again and again her excitement reached a height she had never dreamt of and she forced her face into a pillow and bit into the soft cloaking fabric to suppress the cries of a pleasure beyond bearing.

Afterwards she was so weak she couldn't move and it was a blessed relief to allow the limp heaviness of her exhausted body to simply slump in the shelter of his cradling arms. For the first time in more months than Tally wanted to count she felt both content and happy and she fell blissfully asleep reassured by that conviction. Everything in her world might be in turmoil but it was a turmoil that felt astonishingly *right*.

Around dawn she wakened with a start and sat up, disorientated. The curtains weren't drawn and morning light was stealing across the furniture in shades of peach and gold. But all that mattered to Tally in that instant was the reality that she was alone. The pillow beside hers was dented but empty; and the sheet was cold when her palm traced an investigative sweep across it. She leapt out of bed as though jet-propelled and paid the price for that impulsive movement, wincing as muscles stretched and complained and an ache between her thighs reminded her all too bluntly of how she had passed the night. It was the work of an instant to snatch up the bedspread and cover her nudity within its shimmering folds.

Tally peered out of the window and saw without surprise that the helicopter was gone because, when she thought about it, she *did* have a dim distant memory of the noise of its take-off at some stage of the night. Sander had slept with her then gone, and she felt gutted, not to mention feeling like the worst female fool since the start of the world. Like a woman in a bad dream, shattered and without any proper objective, she wandered down to the ground floor, stiffening in dismay when she heard a noise coming from the kitchen and almost retreating back upstairs again. A cleaner? Housekeeper? After all, both the flower arrangements and the level of cleanliness made it obvious that the house was being efficiently looked after.

A dark head appeared in the doorway and Sander, an impressive bronzed figure clad only in form-fitting silk boxers, gazed up at her with glittering dark eyes of enquiry.

'I thought I heard something. I *thought*...' But she bit back the remains of such a revealing admission, determined to save face. 'I wondered where you were.'

'I was making breakfast,' Sander announced with staggering cool as if it were something he did on a regular basis rather than an entirely new departure for him.

Unshaven, hair still springy and damp from a shower, Sander looked as drop-dead gorgeous as a glossy tiger on the prowl. But no four-legged animal could have sported his muscular six-pack and long powerful thighs. Her heart was racing, her tummy flipping as she moved instinctively closer. 'Breakfast?'

'Just toast and coffee,' he declared in case she might be at risk of expecting something more ambitious, which, with his track record, was most unlikely.

As she padded into the spacious kitchen diner she picked up on the smell of charred toast in the air. The windows were wide open, presumably to clear the lingering fug of smoke. 'The toaster here is rubbish,' Sander proclaimed in exasperation.

He made coffee so black and strong it was like treacle and it would upset her stomach, she reflected ruefully; he couldn't cook, either—he couldn't cook to save his life. He *thought* he could cook but his tools or his ingredients always let him down, whether it was a faulty oven timer or temperature gauge or a tough cut of meat. Convinced that any idiot could cook, he had no patience and was prone to taking disastrous shortcuts. She could picture what had happened this morning: he would have stood over the 'faulty' toaster and cancelled the operation because he couldn't be bothered waiting for the toast to pop up on its own time. Then, when the bread was partially done, he probably had put it in the toaster again and it had burned. But Tally was touched that he was making what she could only interpret as a romantic effort on her behalf, even if his attempt to give her breakfast in bed was more likely to burn the house down.

'I'm not very hungry,' she said, trying to be helpful because the toaster was sending up a warning plume of smoke again and she crossed the kitchen to switch it off before it could set off the fire alarm.

Sander pulled her back into the heat of his big powerful body and growled, 'I'm only hungry for you—we shared a fantastic night, *moli mou*.'

Her memory leapfrogged in some discomfiture over the dynamic night of intimacy that they had shared. He had been insatiable, while she had been wildly, encouragingly responsive to his every move and he had made a lot of them. Indeed his seemingly limitless hunger for her body has struck her as distinctly gratifying when she considered the number of options he had to have as a single male soon to be in full repossession of his freedom. But was very satisfying sex enough to power a reconciliation? Was such a far-reaching idea as ditching their divorce petition even on his mind? With Sander it didn't pay to make assumptions because he was not predictable, nor was he particularly conventional.

A stray thought came out of nowhere and assailed Tally. Reacting to it, she tugged free of him and yanked open the refrigerator, staring in at the packed shelves of fresh produce with wide suspicious eyes. While she mulled over that thought she poured two glasses of fresh orange juice and handed him one. 'Have you been renting this place out?'

'Of course not,' Sander asserted with hauteur. 'I don't want strangers here. This was our home.'

There was only one other explanation for that very well-stocked fridge and it struck Tally like a wake-up call that blew away the cobwebs of a night in which she had enjoyed very little sleep. As she drank her orange juice her brain was suddenly functioning again. Her smooth brow furrowing, green eyes wide with suspicion, she flipped round to study his lean darkly handsome face. 'Did you set me up for this?'

Sander quirked a winged ebony brow. 'What are you talking about?'

And, that fast, Tally knew that Sander had flown to France with an agenda and that she had been seduced to plan within an inch of her life. 'You *planned* to see me here, you even *planned* to spend the night here with me and you set the scene—that's why there are flowers everywhere and the kitchen has been stocked with food.'

'Would you have preferred to have gone hungry? Or to have slept in a damp bed?' Sander enquired in bewilderment, clearly not seeing what all the fuss was about. 'We could hardly stay in comfort in a house that has been empty for so long. Of course I had it prepared for our occupation.'

'You're so devious. How am I supposed to feel about this set-up? I was entrapped!' Tally flung at him furiously.

Brilliant dark golden eyes wary, Sander heaved a sigh and spread lean brown hands in a wholly unconvincing expression of innocence. 'You're my wife and I want you back. That's not a set-up or a crime…'

*I want you back.* Not at all sure yet how she felt about

# CHAPTER THREE

BUT mere minutes after Tally's fiery exit, Sander stepped into the shower cubicle with her, bold as brass as he always was in a challenging situation.

Before she could react, he caught her wet slippery body to his and plunged his mouth down on her angrily parted lips. And what she might have said was forgotten when she did not get the chance to say it. Indeed, it did cross her mind that, although they might have spent many hours together during their marriage, they had shared very few verbal exchanges. But then Sander had always been a man of action and, equally, a man of few words. She acknowledged this dizzily, her hormones surging up with greedy enthusiasm to interfere with such clear-minded thoughts.

In the aftermath of that sizzling bout of lovemaking in the shower, Sander held her close while she tried to persuade her legs to hold her up without his support. Still breathing heavily, he lifted a thick strand of dripping straight hair to ask in bewilderment, 'Why isn't it curling again now that it's wet?'

His mystified expression provoked a spontaneous laugh from Tally. 'I had a special straightening treatment done at a salon and it won't curl again for months now. It's much easier to handle,' she told him brightly.

Releasing that recalcitrant strand from his fingers, Sander stared down at her with a very masculine frown of incomprehension. 'Let it go back to normal,' he urged. 'I loved your hair the way it was…'

Tally was amazed. He had *loved* the corkscrew curls that were the bane of her life? Well, he had never mentioned the fact before. The water was running cool. Switching it off, Sander thrust back the shower doors. As she stepped out he enveloped her in a big fleecy towel. It awakened reminders of the way he had quietly taken care of her in the later stages of her pregnancy when her body had grown heavy and clumsy, restricting her ease of movement. That extra degree of consideration had seemed to come so naturally to him that it had made her heart sing with hope for their future as a new family. And then cruel fate had struck down her fond hopes with tragedy. When their little son had been born dead, let down by placental insufficiency, the hope of them becoming a family had perished with their child and their marriage had followed suit.

Stunning, heavily lashed dark golden eyes resting on her troubled face, Sander tugged her back to him with hands that would not be denied. 'I want to forget the past eighteen months.'

An uneasy laugh fell from her lips. 'It's not that simple.'

His strong jaw line squared. 'It can be as simple as we want it to be. We are the only two people involved here, *moli mou*.'

Sander wanted her back. Maybe he had set her up by inviting her to the house and arriving when she wasn't expecting him, but seemingly he had done so with good intentions. Here she was and, in her own opinion, she wasn't beautiful, wealthy or even particularly talented. But Sander, who enjoyed every one of those worldly advantages, still wanted *her* back as his wife. That was a truth that could only flatter Tally and it reminded her once more of his eagerness to make love to her again.

And Tally's mouth opened, strong curiosity sending words to her lips before she had even taken the time to think them through and question whether or not she might be asking something without being properly prepared for the answer she might receive. 'If I thought that you hadn't been with anyone else since we parted, maybe I could consider that possibility,' she dared to suggest.

A deathly silence fell in which her words hung like a precariously balanced pane of glass ready to drop and noisily shatter. The instant she looked up at Sander she knew that her fond hopes had roamed dangerously far from the truth. His bronzed skin tone could not hide the fact that in receipt of that declaration he had lost colour, his classic cheekbones prominent beneath his brown skin, his wide sensual mouth clenching into a troubled line.

Sander was rigid with heated incredulity, as Tally's need for that assurance had come at him out of nowhere and far too late in the day to have any value to him. It was also a cautionary reminder that Tally's apparent spontaneity and lack of calculation could be misleading

because there was often far more going on below the
surface than she was prepared to acknowledge. And she
had just placed a deadly explosive tripwire right in his
path and he fiercely resented the fact. What right had
she to ask him that now? In the circumstances it was
unreasonable. More than eighteen months ago, Tally
had barred him from her bed and turned her back very
firmly on him as a husband. Refusing even to admit
that their problems might still have a remedy, she had
walked out on their marriage. She had made it clear
that she wasn't coming back and that she wanted a divorce. Furthermore she had excluded him from every
one of those decisions. The period that had followed
their break-up was a blurred black hole of deeply unwelcome memories for Sander, a reality that he was too
proud to even consider sharing with her.

'I'm afraid I can't tell you what you seem to want
to hear,' Sander delivered in a grudging undertone, his
discomfiture patent.

It was Tally's turn to pale and the fierce tension made
her tummy roll with nausea. For a disturbing instant she
just wanted to burst into distraught tears at having received confirmation of what she now knew she had most
feared. She was intensely mortified. What on earth had
possessed her? She felt unbelievably stupid and naïve for
ever having dreamt that Sander might not have sought
sexual solace while they were living apart and divorcing.
Where had her wits been while she entertained such an
unlikely possibility? Sander was, and always had been,
a very sexual being.

'I don't want to know any more,' she told him starkly,

turning away in outright physical rejection, clutching the towel round her trembling body with defensive hands. Her skin was clammy with shock while she struggled to suppress the most destructive wave of sick and bitter jealousy that she had ever experienced. In the space of seconds she had travelled from revived feelings of tenderness to pungent acrimonious hatred. Lost in grief for their infant son, she had fled back to England with a broken heart to lick her wounds and rebuild her life as a single woman while Sander had evidently *partied* and shared his beautiful body with a range of new lovers.

'You're not being fair,' Sander murmured flatly, recognising that judgement was being meted out without further debate.

'Perhaps not…but I can't help how I feel,' Tally responded in a cold tone of finality and mentally she was already shutting up shop on the events of the past twenty-four hours.

She had made yet another mistake but not an insuperable one, she reasoned in the first frantic surge of needing to sort her tumultuous emotions out before they swallowed her alive and destroyed her. Over the past year she had fought hard to regain her independence and overcome her heartache and she was determined not to revisit those dark days of depression and self-doubt. It wasn't that unusual for husbands and wives on the brink of divorce to have one final reunion, she told herself urgently. She had mistaken familiarity for attraction and echoes of the love she had once felt for Sander had clearly confused her. She'd made a mistake, nothing more, nothing less. She didn't need to make a

production out of it and she didn't need to flail herself
for her stupidity either. Sander was a heartstoppingly
handsome and sexy man and a long period of celibacy
had probably made her more vulnerable.

'We just did something very silly,' she muttered, picking up clothes that she had been packing the evening
before and sifting through them to find a fresh outfit to
wear.

'No, we did not,' Sander contradicted with fierce
conviction and then, thinking about what she had said
and how she had reacted to his honesty, he frowned.
'Are you telling me that you haven't slept with Robert
Miller?'

'I'm not telling you anything!' Tally shot back, refusing to be drawn on that topic and wishing she had had
enough sense not to put such a revealing weapon within
his reach. Were he to realise that her relationship with
the other man remained platonic he would soon guess
that she had moved on less smoothly than he had from
their break-up and she could not bear to admit that truth
to him. It was the wrong moment for her to appreciate
that in her heart she had still felt married and loyal to
Sander Volakis. 'I won't even discuss such a thing...'

'But while practising your usual double standards,
it was all right to put *me* on the spot,' Sander traded
harshly and then he groaned out loud as though he regretted the tone of that response and, with a bitten-off
curse, he reached for her small hands instead. 'Tally...
come here...'

Rage suddenly lanced through Tally like a jet-
propelled rocket and her green eyes flashed like

emeralds. 'Don't touch me!' she snapped, trailing her fingers pointedly free of his hold.

'Obviously I should have lied when you asked me that question but that's not my style.' His long, lean, powerful body rigid, Sander cornered her and closed lean brown hands to her elbows instead of her hands. His dark eyes were bright with angry frustration. 'I won't let you do this to us. You still want me.'

'No, I don't. I don't know what came over me—this was a mistake, meeting you here in this house again was like stepping into a time slip!' Tally protested vehemently, desperate to make him believe that for the sake of her pride.

He watched her jerky movements as she dressed in front of him, disdaining a bra in her haste to cover up again. Against his will, his gaze was drawn by the bounce of her full rose-tipped breasts as she hauled on a T-shirt and even after the night they had shared the tightening at his groin was automatic. He didn't want to listen to her spouting rubbish about mistakes and time slips. He didn't want her to leave. Not only did he want his wife back, but he also wanted to keep her in bed for at least a week in the hope of sating a craving that no other woman could come close to satisfying.

'The hunger is still there between us, *moli mou*,' Sander growled. 'As strong as ever...'

His dark deep drawl vibrated down her taut spinal cord and she glanced up from below feathery lashes and connected warily with hot golden eyes that challenged her. Her nipples tingled and swelled and she froze in disbelief that she could still be so susceptible to his allure.

'You know exactly what I'm talking about,' Sander pronounced with satisfaction.

But Tally was determined not to listen. Convinced that the more heed she paid him, the more likely it was that she would do something foolish again, she was determined to escape. Flipping the case that she had begun packing the day before open again, she began to settle a pile of garments into it.

'You can't just walk away and pretend this didn't happen,' Sander breathed levelly.

'I can do whatever I blasted well want!' Tally flared back, shooting his lean, strong profile a defiant glance.

Raking impatient fingers through his black, spiky hair, Sander dealt her a narrow-eyed intent appraisal. His dark eyes, sharp as knives, brought goose flesh up on her bare arms in spite of the warm temperature. 'One way or another I'll get you back, *yineka mou.*'

'I don't think so,' Tally fielded flatly, her small face stiff with self-discipline as she flipped down the lid on the case and closed it. 'We'll be divorced in a couple of months. I don't want anything else from this place. This is the past and I've moved on—'

'Only an hour ago you were happily reliving that past,' Sander murmured, smooth as silk.

'Everybody makes mistakes and you're mine,' Tally retorted curtly, heading for the door as fast as her legs would carry her.

Sander intercepted her and removed the case from

her hold to carry it downstairs for her. 'A mistake you evidently enjoyed repeating,' he traded softly.

Guilty colour ran like a banner into her cheeks as she locked the case into the boot of the car outside. Tormenting images of Sander with other women were playing over and over again inside her head, acting like a refined sort of torture on her vulnerable mind. Mounting distress at those wounding inner pictures made her hand shake as she searched for her keys in her bag.

Frowning down at her, because he was an observant man, Sander rested a lean hand on the driver's door. 'Are you sure that you're feeling well enough to drive?'

'I'm perfectly fine.' Annoyed that she had not contrived to fool him with her façade of calm, Tally jumped into the car without further ado, terrified that she might betray her insecurity in other ways.

'You're running away again, just like you did when you walked out on our marriage,' Sander condemned bleakly.

'I'm being sensible!' Tally contradicted in fierce disagreement and slammed the door shut.

As she drove off she refused to allow herself a backward glance at his tall powerful figure in the driving mirror. That would have been surrendering to weakness and she was ashamed enough of her behaviour over the past twelve hours to feel that she *had* to withstand even that minor temptation.

All the while she was thinking of the many times in her life when she'd had to be tough and control emotions that seemed stronger than those of other people. When she was still a child she had often longed for unconditional love from those close to her. Binkie, of course, had loved Tally, but even at a young age Tally had appreciated that Binkie was in a different category as an employee, a housekeeper and childminder, paid by Tally's mother to do a job. Either the people Tally loved did not have the capacity to love that strongly or she herself did not have the special *je ne sais quoi* that inspired that depth of feeling in others. Yet she knew that when she loved people *she* loved with her whole heart and usually got badly hurt.

The most important person in her mother's, Crystal's, world, however, was generally the current man in her life. But then Crystal Spencer was very much a man's woman and as mother and daughter shared few interests both women had learned to compromise in their expectations of each other. Equally, Tally's father, Anatole, had always made it obvious that he was ashamed of his elder daughter's illegitimate birth and, since he was a man to whom appearances meant a great deal, he had never been prepared to openly acknowledge her as his child. The feelings of his current wife, who had long preferred to pretend Tally didn't exist, were much more important to him.

Had that unfortunate background encouraged her to look for too much support and attention from Sander? Tally asked herself suddenly. Had she been too needy in their relationship? Had she expected too much from a young man thrust into marriage and parenthood when he had not, at first, chosen to freely embrace either? Her ruminations about her marriage always seemed to return to the same cruel fact: when Tally had fallen pregnant her father had blackmailed Sander into marrying her by threatening the stability of Volakis Shipping. Even though Sander had later insisted that he wanted to stay married to Tally, the truth of the terms on which their marriage had initially been built was a humiliation that could never be ignored or forgotten.

Yet she had loved Sander so much in those days that she had closed her eyes to the flaws in their relationship. He had not loved her, nor had he pretended to do so. He had wanted her, supported her, cared for her, entertained her in and out of bed, but he had never felt for her the depth of emotion that she had felt for him. And that heart-rending truth had ensured that right from the start Tally felt like the lesser and weaker partner in their marriage.

With every kilometre of French autoroute that she travelled along, taking her further and further from Sander, Tally was increasingly conscious of a tight, funny ache inside that felt remarkably like the pain of intense loss. She suppressed the sensation, fighting its worrying pull on her disordered senses. That was only her imagination overreacting, she told herself impatiently.

But why was Sander so keen to get her back? Her tough Greek husband was such a macho guy. Was it simply his possessive streak? Was he like a dog with a discarded bone he wanted nobody else to touch? Had his belief that she was now with Robert Miller powered Sander's desire to reclaim his wife? It was a desire that astonished her, for she knew his parents had probably heaved a sigh of relief when their son's marriage failed.

She had not impressed her snobbish in-laws as an acceptable wife for their only surviving son. Her illegitimacy and downmarket background had offended them. When she and Sander had still been happy together, his parents' attitude had seemed unimportant because, aside of Petros Volakis working with Sander in the family business, the older couple had taken very little interest in their son or his wife during their brief marriage. Nor had they attended the sad little funeral for their infant grandchild, choosing to send only a card expressing conventional regret.

While Tally waited to board the ferry at the cross-channel port, she realised that she was looking forward to the prospect of her mother's company in London because she was in no mood to be on her own. What had happened with Sander, however, she resolved to keep entirely to herself. Fortunately, she was not so involved with Robert that she owed him any kind of an explanation either. The less time she spent agonising over events that she could not change, the happier she would be, she decided doggedly.

Unfortunately, when Tally returned to London she found her mother to be in a brittle, evasive mood and more interested in looking up all her old friends than spending time with her only child. Just a week later, however, Tally called in at her apartment to pick up a colour swatch she had forgotten and walked into the midst of an astonishing scene. A stockily built older man in a suit was telling her sobbing mother that tears weren't going to change anything…

'What the heck is going on here?' Tally demanded on the threshold of the room.

Wild-eyed, Crystal flung her a daughter a startled look and, emitting a strangled sob, she scrambled upright and fled into her bedroom without another word.

In bewilderment Tally directed her attention to her mother's visitor instead. 'Maybe you could tell me what this is about?'

'I'm afraid that I'm not at liberty to do so. This is a very confidential matter,' the older man responded starchily as he lifted his briefcase and headed for the door. 'I've left my contact details on the table. Perhaps when Miss Spencer has had the chance to consider her options she will call me.'

Mystified, Tally saw him out and then sped back into the lounge to lift his business card and frown down at it: *Henry Fellows.* He was a solicitor and she had never heard of him before. Rapping her knuckles lightly on the door of the guest room, Tally went in.

Standing by the window with defensively folded arms, her mother shot her an apprehensive glance from reddened eyes. 'Has he gone yet?'

'Yes, he's gone. What did he want with you?'

Crystal's slim shoulders drooped. 'I might as well tell you because you'll find out soon enough. Roger is threatening me with the police.'

Aghast, Tally stared at the older woman. 'The... *police*? Roger? What on earth are you talking about?'

The story that Crystal began to tell was not entirely unexpected. Over the years, Tally's mother had often got into financial trouble and Tally was not surprised to learn that the older woman had been in debt when she first moved in with the retired businessman, Roger Tailford, in Monaco.

'At the beginning I managed to keep up payments on what I owed out of the allowance that Roger gave me for clothes.'

'Couldn't you have told Roger the truth?' Tally asked ruefully.

'Roger was very puritanical about money and I knew he would think less of me if he ever found out, so I kept it a secret,' Crystal admitted grudgingly. 'But then the interest kept on rising and the payments got steeper so I was desperate for more money…and one day I forged Roger's signature on a cheque and managed to cash it. He insisted on still using cheques—he was very old-fashioned that way. He didn't hold with debit cards, online banking and the like…'

Tally was studying the tear-stained older woman fixedly. 'Did you say that you *forged* Roger's signature on a cheque? That's a crime!'

'I'm not stupid. I know that, but it kept the peace between Roger and I and he was so well-off he never missed the money…'

'Are you saying that you did it more than once?' Tally pressed in horror.

'I was in debt to my eyeballs!' Crystal cried defensively. 'I had to keep the creditors away from the door somehow!'

'But it was stealing! Surely you can see that?' her daughter challenged her. 'You were *stealing* from Roger! Why was that solicitor here?'

'Roger's accountant questioned some of the cheques and Roger found out what I'd done. That's why we broke up—he threw me out!' Crystal sobbed. 'He sent the solicitor here to tell me that he won't prosecute me for the forged cheques if I repay all the money I took.'

Tally was ashen pale. 'How much money are we talking about?'

Her mother mentioned a sum that made Tally gasp: it was a *much* larger sum than she might have expected. Having got away with her initial theft, Crystal had become bolder and had begun dipping into Roger's account whenever she had overspent or needed more money. In the course of two years she had helped herself to a pretty substantial amount of cash. Tally was appalled by the total.

'Are you able to pay back anything?' Tally asked worriedly, a look of hope in her eyes.

'I haven't a penny,' Crystal confessed dully. 'I've never had savings. You know that.'

'Well, when it comes to ready cash, I can't help you. What I have is in the business and I'm bound by my partnership with Robert to leave it there,' Tally volunteered unhappily. 'And in the current economic climate, I'll never get a loan for that amount. There's only one thing for it: we'll have to ask my father for help—'

'Don't waste your time. Anatole would probably love it if I was sent to prison for theft.'

That night, when Tally phoned her father, she was relieved that he didn't laugh when she told him about her mother's predicament, but he didn't sound sympathetic either. 'Why don't you approach your husband for assistance? Oh, yes, I forgot. You got bored with him and walked out on your marriage…'

Smarting at his sarcasm, Tally muttered, 'It wasn't like that.'

But it was very clear that Anatole wasn't interested in hearing her side of that story. As far as he was concerned, when he had put pressure on Sander to wed his daughter because she was pregnant he had helped Tally make a 'good' marriage and in leaving her husband she had recklessly thrown away her golden opportunity.

'Look, I'll be in London on Wednesday,' he told her abruptly. 'I'll meet you for lunch at the usual place. One o'clock.'

And with that unanticipated invitation, Tally had to be content while she wondered if there was any real prospect of her father offering his help in order to save Crystal from what he would undoubtedly see as her just deserts. She was well aware of how much her father had resented having to maintain Crystal throughout the years of his older daughter's childhood. When she got back from a day spent working out a new interior scheme for a client who was infuriatingly given to changing her mind every five minutes, she found her mother sitting in floods of tears at the kitchen table.

'That solicitor phoned: Roger is planning to call in the police on Monday. That's my deadline,' Crystal advanced in tremulous explanation, fastening frightened eyes to her daughter's frowning face. 'Oh, Tally, what am I going to do? Your father will never help me. He probably just invited you to lunch so that he can hear the dirty details and gloat.'

'Let's hope for the best,' Tally responded, grimacing at the reality that her parents so thoroughly disliked each other. Though she'd had an affair while she was engaged to and pregnant by Anatole, Crystal had pursued Anatole through the courts to receive maintenance for their daughter. In any case, Tally had never known her father to act out of compassion. Anatole Karydas was first and foremost a businessman and he hadn't made money out of being a soft touch. On the other hand, he was the only hope Crystal had, Tally reflected unhappily: she could scarcely approach Sander for financial help while she was pursuing a divorce he had said he didn't want.

'I've got a proposition to put to you,' Anatole, a small portly man with iron-grey hair and shrewd dark eyes, informed his daughter within minutes of her joining him at his table at his favourite Italian restaurant. 'I'll give you the money for Crystal, no questions asked, but only if you agree to go back and live with your husband.'

Completely taken aback by that offer, which had come out of nowhere, Tally froze, her eyes very wide. 'You've got to be joking!'

'I don't joke about serious matters. I valued having a connection to the Volakis tribe—they're very important well-connected people in Athens—'

'How can that influence you? Nobody there even knows that I'm your daughter.'

Anatole compressed his lips in disagreement. 'A lot of my friends and business colleagues know about you now. Sander's parents let the cat out of the bag, so you're not a secret any more. And why should you be?' he remarked in a sudden burst of irritation that took her aback. 'I would be very happy to see you go back to live with your husband.'

'That's ridiculous—'

'No, it's not, it's sensible and still the best option you have,' he contradicted with conviction. 'I don't want you ending up like your mother, living off one man and then another, until you end up in the gutter and start stealing to get by. I want my daughter to enjoy a normal decent life, and Sander Volakis can give you that.'

Tally was shattered by that little speech because it had never once in all the years she had known her father occurred to her that he might cherish a genuine concern for her well-being. Certainly he had never revealed such an interest in her welfare before. Green eyes reflecting her surprise, she stared at the older man with a frown building between her brows.

'I know I've not been a proper father to you, that I've made mistakes and let my dislike of your mother and my respect for my wife's wishes come between us,' Anatole admitted grittily, evading her startled scrutiny. 'But I won't stand by and watch you burn your boats with Sander Volakis if I can help it. So, if you want that money to save Crystal's worthless skin, you can have it, but you have to give your marriage another chance for at least a year.' He hesitated. 'What happened with your child was tragic but, given time, you'll get over it and start again.'

Shaken, Tally felt her eyes sting with hot tears at that blunt reference. 'Sander's parents didn't seem to care…'

Her father touched her hand in a brief awkward gesture and then looked away, his discomfiture obvious in the humming silence. But it was clear to her that even though he did not have the words he had felt a good deal more than Sander's parents when he'd learned of her stillborn son, who would have been his first grandchild. 'Well, will you accept my offer?'

Wildly disconcerted by a choice she had never envisaged, Tally said thinly that she couldn't make up her mind there and then. Ironically, although she was furious that Anatole was trying to manipulate her now as he had once manipulated Sander, she could not help feeling touched that her father was concerned in his own way about her future. And how *could* she stand back and allow her mother to be charged and possibly even imprisoned for fraud? The law came down hard on women who were dishonest with money, she acknowledged worriedly, particularly a spoiled woman like Crystal who had not held down a paying job in more years than her daughter cared to count. Tally also knew that her mother could not be allowed to go on running up debts that she couldn't afford while struggling to maintain a lifestyle that she should have abandoned years earlier. She was painfully aware at that moment that *she* would have to instigate changes in Crystal's life in return for advancing Anatole's money. To ignore the roots of Crystal's problem would be to invite the same situation to happen again.

'Yes…I'll accept,' Tally finally conceded in a tense undertone. She refused to think in any depth about the marriage that she was agreeing to return to and simply accepted that she was putting her pride and independence on a funeral pyre.

She couldn't face phoning Sander and hearing the triumph edge his slow dark drawl, so she texted him like a teenager determined to avoid confrontation.

*Have changed my mind. Willing to try being married again.*

Sander phoned her while she was waiting for her mother to return from a shopping trip. 'I'll pick you up for dinner—'

'No…er…I'm busy tonight. Mum's staying with me at present,' she explained hurriedly. 'I'll pack and see you tomorrow at the apartment—'

'I sold the apartment last year and bought a house.' Sander reeled off the address, his Greek accent roughening every vowel sound. 'Tally…you won't regret this.'

Momentarily, Tally was discomfited. Sander had assumed that she was returning to him of her own free will. That was far from being the case but she saw no good reason to admit the ugly truth. What would it achieve? She was methodically packing her things when Crystal came home. Joining the older woman in the lounge, she was quick to share the news that her father was willing to settle Crystal's debt to Roger.

Crystal was stunned. 'I never thought Anatole would play the good Samaritan.'

'There's a price—for both of us. I had to agree to give my marriage another go,' Tally volunteered. 'And, before we go any further, you have to agree to get a job.'

'A *job*?' Crystal gasped in ringing disbelief. 'What on earth would I do?'

'You won't find out until you try. Maybe you could work in the beauty or cosmetics fields…I don't know exactly what you'd do but, whatever, you need to get a job and earn enough money to keep yourself.'

'I couldn't!'

'Of course you can. You don't need another man to keep you. You'll have no credit card bills to worry about this time around. We'll cut the cards up and you'll do what other people do: live on a budget, not beyond your means.'

Crystal blinked. 'You're out of your mind.'

'No, I'm telling you the only way that this will work for you. This—Anatole coming to the rescue—is a once-in-a-lifetime deal,' Tally was careful to stress. 'It's going to be tough for you to make a fresh start and leave old habits behind, but you're stronger than you think. Things have to change. You can't go on spending money you don't have.'

'Well, I could, if my wealthy daughter chose to help me out,' Crystal dared with more than a hint of her usual calculation.

'No, I'm not going to ask Sander to foot all your bills. That wouldn't be fair,' Tally fielded unhappily. 'Isn't it enough that I'm being forced to return to a marriage I had already turned my back on?'

'You can't fool me,' Crystal breathed witheringly. 'I don't believe you'll ever turn your back willingly on Sander Volakis. He's the love of your life!'

Crystal remained in an edgy, sharp-tongued mood as

she fought the prospect of being self-supporting; but, by the end of the evening, Tally had secured her agreement to seek employment and felt satisfied with that climb-down as a first step in a new lifestyle.

The next day, Robert was astonished when Tally brought him up to speed on events. 'You're going back to live with Sander Volakis? Since when?'

'When we met at the house in France he asked me to give our marriage another chance,' Tally admitted tautly. 'I've thought about it and I've decided he's right—'

'But he's *wrong*!' Robert Miller protested in sudden anger. 'You were unhappy with him.'

'Things only went wrong between us after we lost our child.'

'But what about us? What about *me*?' Robert demanded feelingly.

'We haven't moved beyond friendship,' Tally reasoned uncomfortably.

'And whose fault is that? You were determined to wait for your divorce to come through!' Robert's blue eyes shone bright with resentment.

Tally's posture became taut because her tender conscience was twanging. 'We still have to work together. Let's not have bad feeling between us.'

'We're business partners and that won't be changing.' Robert swore with unnecessary vehemence. 'You can tell Volakis from me that there's no way I'll ever allow him to buy me out of Tallulah Design!'

After that emotional confrontation, which left Tally wondering unhappily if she was guilty of having misled Robert, she felt utterly wrung out...

# CHAPTER FOUR

AT SEVEN that evening, Tally arrived with her luggage at Sander's town house.

It was a very large and imposing property, traditionally furnished, not at all like his previous slick, contemporary apartment, she recalled. It also struck her as very much a family home rather than the archetypal single man's pad. Sander was still at work, which set her teeth on edge, resurrecting as it did unfortunate memories of the past when he had rarely been available when she wanted him to be. Avoiding the bedroom that he clearly occupied, Tally chose another. They might be getting back together but that didn't mean they had to live in each other's pockets straight away, she reasoned. In fact the prospect of a little distance while she got used to the idea of behaving like a wife again was very appealing to Tally.

After a more than usually demanding day at the London headquarters of Volakis Shipping, Sander was unusually keen to get home.

Tally dressed with care for her first meal in Sander's company, choosing a colourful floral dress that skimmed her slim thighs and lovingly moulded her breasts. When she heard the slam of the front door she stood up, her heart fluttering like a wild thing in her chest, and waited on the threshold of the elegant drawing room into which the housekeeper had shown her.

Sheathed in a dark business suit, black hair tousled by the breeze, his strong jaw line roughened by a day's stubble, Sander gazed steadily back at her. In her opinion the only word that matched him at that moment was *beautiful*. He had the sleek dark beauty of a glossy predator, she recognised, every sense sent spinning by his charismatic punch. He studied her from black fringed deep-set dark eyes, as usual defying her expectations with his low-key response to her presence in his home.

'Are you hungry?' he asked her eventually and her tummy flipped, sexual awareness snaking through her in a twisting, fast-flowing river. That quickly she found out how switched on she still was to Sander's every look and word. Warm colour rose to her cheeks, her nipples tingling into tautness as she pressed her slender thighs together in a pointless effort to contain the ache he had stirred up.

'No, for once you mistake me,' Sander purred, the dark intonation of his deep drawl recognising the sensual nature of her tension, his instant awareness warning her how easily he could read her. 'I'm not that much of a philistine. We'll eat, *talk…*'

'I picked a guest room,' Tally told him, keen to get that fact out there before there was a misunderstanding.

'Not a problem, assuming you are not planning to

stay there for ever,' Sander fielded equably. 'I'm a patient man.'

'You didn't used to be.'

His golden gaze locked to hers and smouldered hot before the thick screen of his lashes shut her out again. 'I want us to stay married. I'll do what I have to do to achieve that, *yineka mou*,' he traded levelly.

His directness impressed her, reminding her that she was hiding behind the myth that she was giving their marriage another go of her own free will. Her cheeks flushed, green eyes strained with discomfiture. 'It won't be easy.'

'Some masochist once said that nothing worth having was easily acquired,' Sander quipped huskily, keen to ease her tension. The fancy dress was overkill for a young woman who thought a dash of perfume equalled formality, so he knew she had made a major effort on his behalf. As he could see how nervous she was he would make no sudden moves. It still hadn't sunk in with Tally, he reflected with pained tenderness, that the only kind of dress he admired was the sort that had no hidden fastenings and came off quickly. He was wholly the philistine he had said he was not, but he would make a major effort to hide the fact.

Tally got into bed that night and slept the instant her head hit the pillow, stress draining away to be replaced by exhaustion. She was back with Sander although they were sleeping apart, but the very fact that he had accepted that without protest let her know how keen he was for their reconciliation to work. Maybe they would eventually have another child, she found herself thinking, but the instant she surrendered to that controversial idea she was gripped by fierce guilt and decided that it was way too soon to be thinking that way. The guilt such an idea evoked still bit deep into her soul. There was no way she would ever seek to replace the little boy she had lost, but even acknowledging that some day they might consider having a family again was a big step for her to make.

A hand shook her shoulder gently and the fringe of her soft lashes lifted on her drowsy eyes. She focused on Sander and the light piercing the curtains behind him. 'Did I sleep in? Am I late for something?'

'No. This is day one of our reconciliation,' Sander reminded her, brilliant dark eyes resting on her flushed face with an intensity he couldn't hide. 'And we're going on holiday.'

'On holiday?' Tally exclaimed in astonishment. 'What on earth...?'

'Sometimes I have good ideas,' Sander intoned lazily. 'We need time to get used to each other again and I don't think we need an audience of friends or family while we do it. I've made arrangements. We fly out at noon.'

'Fly where?' Tally demanded, sitting up and pushing her tousled hair out of her eyes. 'Where are we going?'

A charismatic smile curved Sander's wide sensual mouth. 'It's a surprise. Everything's organised. You don't even need to pack.'

'How can I not need to pack?' Tally queried in exasperation, regretting the reality that most of the clothes she owned for a warmer climate were still stored in France.

'Because I've asked a friend to send a selection of beach wear in your size to the villa we'll be using. I don't want you having to fuss about what to take—it puts you in such a bad mood,' Sander murmured teasingly.

'How long will we be away?' Tally demanded. 'Sander, I have a business to run, and appointments, clients…'

Sander rested a fingertip gently against her parted lips to silence her, his dark eyes gleaming gold as he surveyed her expectantly. 'Just this once put *us* first. This time around I intend to. Clients come and go just like business deals. Marriages are a little more fragile. We have a window of opportunity here, so let's make the most of it while we can, *moli mou*.'

And as Sander took his leave Tally was amazed that he was willing to make so much of an effort to give their marriage the time and space to find a firm footing again. He was an out and out workaholic and if he was prepared to put her ahead of business she could do no less for him. Galvanised into action, she scrambled out of bed and called Belle, her assistant, to inform her that she was going away. Together the two women ran through her appointments, deciding which could be rescheduled for her return or selected for a video-conferencing consultation instead.

Clad in a simple green linen shift dress and having packed only an overnight bag, Tally headed for the airport with a surprisingly light heart and a sense of suppressed excitement that made her blush like a teenager when she boarded the Volakis jet and met her husband's steady dark gaze. He did have the most beautiful dark eyes, she conceded, and the reflection exasperated her, tightening her facial muscles as she exerted steely control over her wandering thoughts. Ever since the end of her marriage Tally had tried to keep strict control of her emotions, for heartbreak had taught her that protecting herself was only common sense. Unfortunately the responses that Sander inspired had always fallen outside the boundaries of what she considered acceptable and run dangerously deep in intensity. Crystal had called Sander the love of Tally's life, a description that she rejected with a strong mental sniff of disagreement.

She no longer loved Sander, she reminded herself with pride. She had got over her broken heart in the aftermath of their marriage. Reality had smashed her illusions when Sander appeared not to share her grief and got on with his life, seemingly untouched by the depression, guilt and vulnerability that had plagued her after the loss of their child. Even though she suspected now that that interpretation was not a fair judgement of how he had felt at the time, she had, nonetheless, learned to live without him and the sensual buzz he carried with him.

Although her father had bribed and bullied her into giving her marriage another chance, she had no intention of allowing herself to forget that she was taking part in what was nothing more than a trial reconciliation. For a year, a little voice yelped in disbelief. Could she live with Sander for an entire year and remain untouched by her emotions? Coolly she reminded herself that Sander had lived with her throughout their marriage without giving way to any of the more tender emotions. He had never once chosen to view good sex and companionship in the high-watt light of love. He had kept his feet on the ground then and this time around *so would she*, Tally assured herself protectively.

'Where are we?' she demanded as they left the plane a few hours later and a hot golden sun in a cloudless blue sky warmed her skin.

'Morocco,' Sander supplied, retrieving their passports from the hovering official and tucking her into the waiting limousine. 'A friend offered me the use of his villa on the Mediterranean coast.'

Tally, who had already made her own deductions from the heat, and the French language Sander had employed to communicate, relaxed in the air-conditioned cool of the limo. As they travelled towards the coast they followed a mountainous route that offered breathtaking views of terraced valleys planted with olive and fruit orchards. The almond trees were in full bloom with fluffy clouds of white blossom. Daylight was fading into dusk when the limousine finally rolled to a halt outside a sprawling white villa surrounded by lush gardens. As Tally stepped out she could hear the rushing sound of the tide hitting the beach somewhere close by and the evocative salty tang of the sea assailed her nostrils.

'Have you been here before?' Tally asked.

'Once, when I was a student in sixth form. I went to school with Alexei Drakos. This property belongs to him,' Sander told her, closing a hand over hers to walk her through the garden.

Tally was reluctantly impressed by that careless reference to one of the world's richest men.

Sander came to a halt at the edge of an infinity pool that overlooked a secluded stretch of golden sand washed by whispering surf. 'It's a fabulous spot. In a perfect world I would have brought you here for our honeymoon.'

Tally thought back ruefully to the early weeks of their marriage when Sander had had to concentrate on saving the family shipping firm rather than on his new marriage. They strolled back towards the villa where they were greeted by a member of staff. Abu wore a long white djellaba. He was very proud of the villa and pleased to have guests to look after. While decorated in traditional style with strong colours, beautiful hand-painted tiles and opulent fabrics, the house was also blessed with every possible luxury and technological extra. Doors and windows opened and curtains closed at the press of a button. A state-of-the-art office sat next door to a master bedroom and en-suite breathtaking marble bathrooms straight out of the *Arabian Nights*.

'You can use these rooms,' Sander pronounced.

After a leisurely and beautifully cooked evening meal Tally made the most of that invitation. She enjoyed a shower in the walk-in wet room and then, clad in a thin cotton wrap, sat out on the wrought-iron balcony that gave a wonderful view of the sea and the mountains. A pretty town sat further round the bay. Mosque minarets and orderly ranks of painted villas encircled the steep hillside behind the harbour. She texted her assistant to let her know her whereabouts, then smothering a yawn, she finally climbed into the wide comfortable divan and closed her eyes, realising that she felt more relaxed than she had done in months. Why was that? Could it be the simple knowledge that Sander was nearby made her feel secure?

When she awoke, a pair of maids was engaged in hanging garments in a capacious wardrobe. Feeling deliciously rested, she got up, bid the smiling young women good morning in her slightly rusty French and examined the clothing that Sander had promised her. The selection of holiday apparel was impressive. Choosing an azure-blue bikini and a beach dress, she went off to freshen up.

Abu greeted her at the foot of the stairs and informed her that flowers had been delivered for her. He showed her the magnificent arrangement of elegant white roses in a tall vase. Smiling with pleasure, Tally walked out onto the terrace where Sander was having breakfast.

'The flowers are gorgeous…thank you,' she said softly.

Ebony brows pleating, Sander glanced up. 'What flowers? I didn't send any,' he declared with a frown.

'Oh…' Tally flushed to the roots of her hair and walked back indoors to take a closer look at the flowers. This time she noticed the small discreet card and plucked it out to peruse it.

'*Thinking about you. Robert.*' Sander read the message over her slim shoulder in a growl of disbelief. 'How dare he!'

Still mortified by her automatic assumption that Sander had sent her the roses, Tally bristled.

'I will tell Abu to dispose of them,' Sander pronounced.

'No, you will not!' Tally objected. 'Why shouldn't Robert send me flowers?'

'It's inappropriate.' Lean strong face set like granite, Sander studied her with angry dark golden eyes. 'You are my wife.'

Tally shrugged off the reminder with a carelessness that was a warning, because she had no intention of getting involved in a petty, macho-male stand-off over a small gift of flowers. She sat down on the terrace to a breakfast of yogurt, fresh fruit and a chocolate-filled croissant of which every bite delivered bliss. By the time she was ready to go for a walk Sander had recovered his temper sufficiently to ditch his glower and accompany her.

They strolled along the empty beach in the sunshine. Tally dug her toes into the silky sand and, ambling down to the water's edge, took off her wrap and paddled with the simple enjoyment of a child.

'We never got the chance to relax like this when we were first married. I was working long hours,' Sander remarked with a roughened edge of regret to his deep dark drawl. 'We'd only been together a few weeks when you fell pregnant, so we didn't know each other that well either—'

'Yes,' Tally acknowledged wryly. 'At the time, I didn't think of it like that, but it was—'

'And then we had to act like adults and I wasn't ready for the responsibility,' he breathed grimly as he gazed out to sea, his introspective mood unusual enough to attract her wondering appraisal.

'You didn't have enough time to get acclimatised to the idea of being a parent.'

His darkened jaw line clenched and he studied her heart-shaped face from below the black fringe of his fabulous long lashes. 'When it came to how I felt about the baby it was more than that…'

When the silence dragged on she turned back to him to encourage him to continue. 'More?'

Sander grimaced, his discomfiture with the subject matter obvious as he hesitated. 'I didn't have a happy childhood. Nobody ill-treated me, I just wasn't a loved or wanted child. I don't know what I did to make it like that. My mother seemed repulsed by me and my father had no time for me either, yet Titos got plenty of attention.' He shrugged a broad shoulder in a surprisingly awkward gesture that didn't quite succeed in dismissing the wounding mystery of his parents' favouritism, as if it was beneath his notice to comment on it.

Tally bit back a feeling flood of sympathy because she could see just how difficult he was finding it to tell her such personal things.

'I was quite young when I decided that I didn't ever want children of my own,' Sander admitted grittily. 'I didn't want to hurt any child the way I had been hurt and I was afraid that whatever was lacking in my parents might be missing in me too.'

Tally was shaken, for it had never occurred to her that he might cherish such deep-seated doubts about his ability to be a good father. She had attributed his reluctance to much more superficial and selfish reactions and she was ashamed of the fact.

'I think…if you'd got the chance,' she muttered awkwardly, 'you would have made a great father. You're not like your parents. I'd be the first to admit that I hardly know them but, from what I have seen of them, they do seem rather cold and detached.'

Absorbing the anxious light in her gaze, Sander gave her a sizzling smile of appreciation. 'You have such a tender heart.'

He bent his proud, dark head and kissed her with a hungry fervour that made her tummy somersault and her knees wobble. Her hands sliding up to his shoulders to steady herself, she stared up at him, her heart thumping as if she had been running. It was a fake reconciliation, she reminded herself doggedly. She didn't want to be married to him any more and she no longer loved him, she truly didn't. But *he* didn't know that and the acknowledgement filled her with guilt, for dishonesty did not come naturally to Tally. His wide sensual mouth found hers again and the world spun on its axis leaving her dizzy. Heat surged in her pelvis, her nipples tightening into taut straining buds. While she was wondering in some shame if she had to love him to sleep with him again, Sander released her from that inner conflict by walking her back up to the pool and suggesting they have a swim. There was not even a hint that he might wish to engage in anything of a more intimate nature.

Two days later the second bouquet of exquisite roses was delivered.

*'Missing you. Robert,'* it said on the accompanying card.

'This is totally out of order!' Sander launched at

Tally, crumpling the card in a strong brown hand while regarding her with a censorious frown.

'Our reconciliation took Robert by surprise,' she confessed uncomfortably. 'He's being deliberately provocative, which is unlike him. But it has to be *my* fault that he feels he was treated badly.'

'What does Miller mean to you?' Sander demanded starkly, dark eyes bright with subdued heat.

Tally was stiff with discomfiture. 'I'm very fond of him but I don't want to talk about him. Now that I'm with you again, everything's changed.'

Although visibly challenged by her reticence, Sander veiled his incisive gaze and compressed his mouth and the subject was dropped. He spent the afternoon teaching her to scuba dive and the day ended with dinner in a restaurant on the quayside overlooking the bay. When they returned to the villa, Abu served them with mint tea and delicate little pastries that melted in the mouth. Sander handed Tally a small leather box.

'I bought it in London. When you feel ready I'd like you to wear it.'

Tally opened the box to reveal a new wedding ring. Taken aback, she paled, giving him an uncertain look.

'Is it too soon?' Raw frustration edged his voice and clenched his strong facial bones. In an abrupt movement he sprang upright and strode to the end of the terrace, glancing back at her, his lean darkly handsome face hard with impatience. 'I'm trying to play by your rules but it goes against the grain. I don't want to be your new best friend, *moli mou*,' he confided bluntly.

Embarrassed and confused by a powerful urge to

throw herself in his arms, Tally cradled the ring box in the palm of her hand, truly shaken by its presentation. It was such a traditional move for a guy who was rarely predictable.

'I want to be your lover, your husband, the father of your second child,' Sander declared huskily.

His declaration sent a quiver of deep longing rippling through Tally. As a lover he was superlative and resisting his powerful charisma became daily more difficult as she was no longer the innocent she had once been. She lay alone in her big bed questioning whether or not she was faking anything with Sander. Certainly she was not faking her enjoyment. He was incredibly good company. He had confided in her about his childhood. That demonstration of trust and his evident intent to do things differently meant a great deal to her when it came from a guy who was resolutely independent and unsentimental and ungiven to self-examination. Once again Sander was becoming the first thing she thought about when she opened her eyes in the morning and the last at night.

The separate bedroom idea had never been designed to run and run. Sander might not be aware of it, but that had been Tally's quiet way of declaring her independence in spite of the manner in which her father had forced her to return to her marriage. But intelligence warned her that it would be unwise to use sex as a reward system when it was always so very easily available in Sander's world. To ignore that salient fact would be very foolish indeed.

*The father of your second child.* His careful acknowledgement of their first child made her eyes sting and she could no longer deny her intense yearning for another baby. There was an empty space inside her that could only be warmed by a child, she acknowledged painfully. Maybe that was the real healing that she needed and before she could change her mind, she scrambled out of bed and crossed the corridor into the room that Sander occupied.

Sander was lying back on the bed, his lean bronzed body sprawled on top of the sheet, watching the business news. He wore only black boxer shorts. His handsome dark head turned, dark golden eyes bright with surprise. But Sander was, as always, a quick study. Powerful muscles flexing, he sat up and extended a hand in invitation. Her heart thumping like a piston engine, she grasped his fingers.

Eyes screened to a golden glimmer by his black lashes, Sander murmured, 'There's no going back from this, *yineka mou*. No half measures.'

It was so typical of Sander's aggressive style to take advantage of a vulnerable moment by laying down conditions that Tally almost laughed. 'All right,' she whispered.

A long finger brushed her still bare wedding finger. 'And tomorrow you put my ring back on and you don't take it off again.'

Tally gazed into his dark deep-set eyes, her heartbeat racing inside her chest. She could not believe his nerve: he was offering her sex only if she signed up for the long-term haul of marriage. If anything showed her how much Sander had matured and changed, that proposition

did. But she had gone back to live with him in return
for her father settling her mother's debts and she had
not thought through what she was doing. Now it was
make-your-mind-up time and she realised in that instant
that she had never had a moment of doubt. There was
only one man in the world who could make her feel as
she felt just then and she couldn't turn away from him,
no matter what the cost of the decision. She still loved
Sander, she still loved him more than she had thought
she could ever love anyone and that was her bottom
line.

Sander leant forward and circled her lush pink lips
with his, very gently but that teasing contact awakened
the fire she had kept banked down inside her and she
shifted, immediately tilting towards him, her hand
rising so that her fingers could lodge in the depths
of his thick close cropped black hair. She kissed him
back passionately and he spread her knees to arrange
her over him. His hand glided up the slender length of
her thigh to caress the slick honey-dewed folds of her
womanhood.

She was already so tender there that hunger flashed
through her like a forking stab of lightning. A flood of
response engulfed her when he rubbed the tiny bud of
her arousal. He pushed a finger into her tight wet sheath
and she gave herself up to sensation, her hands clutching at his hair and his shoulders, her womb contracting
with excitement. The waves of desire came faster and
faster as her hips squirmed. She came with explosive
intensity in an erotic release that went on and on and
on and long before it had finished Sander had divested

himself of his boxers and pushed into her slick wet heat with forceful male energy.

He felt so unbelievably good she breathed urgently, 'Don't stop!'

'I won't.' His hands anchored to her hips to control the pace of their lovemaking, Sander ground his body into hers so that she writhed in ecstasy, her body incredibly sensitive to his every movement. With superb sensual timing he lifted her and brought her down again. Catching his primal rhythm, she rejoiced in every ravishing plunge of his strong male body up into hers. Excitement hurtled through her like an express train, racing faster and faster. Suddenly it was a challenge to breathe and as he shuddered under her with an uninhibited shout of satisfaction her body convulsed again and the world splintered around her.

'I didn't use a condom,' Sander gasped, struggling to catch his breath.

Tally smiled dreamily against a satin smooth brown shoulder and went totally limp in acceptance. 'That's all right.'

The following day she staged a couple of video conferences with new clients and then left the office free for Sander's use and spent the afternoon engaged in sketching out preliminary designs. For the first time in more months than she cared to count she felt free and happy and she knew she owed that renewed zest for life and sense of completeness to being with Sander again.

In the month that followed that contentment only deepened for Tally. Most weekends they spent a couple of days staying in a hotel in Marrakesh where they visited art galleries, dined at fashionable restaurants and mingled at trendy clubs. During the week they fell into a routine of working long-distance several hours every morning at their respective jobs, sharing the office facilities with only occasional clashes. They went scuba diving, walked in the oak forests and explored tiny isolated villages in the mountains where time seemed to have stopped somewhere around a century earlier. When they felt lazier they relaxed by the pool and picnicked on the beach. They became lovers again, easy in each other's company, touching without a questioning look to see if the approach was welcome, comfortable with the silences.

By the time they returned to London, their reconciliation had lasted six weeks and Tally was already secretly nourishing the hope that she might have conceived again…

made him the sole beneficiary of her estate. Apparently his presence was urgently required in Paris.

Sander suppressed a groan of disbelief. He had at least a dozen questions to ask but the French lawyer had already ended the call, having extracted Sander's assurance that he would come as soon as possible to Paris. Why the hell would Oleia have left him anything at all? And could there be a worse case of bad timing? Out of the blue Tally had come back to him, their marriage was back on track and the very last thing Sander felt he needed was a shadowy link cast by a past lover. And, of all women, Oleia—whom Tally had more reason than she knew to be sensitive about, Sander reflected ruefully, his brilliant dark eyes clouding with grudging recollection. Oleia, exotic and flighty as a hummingbird, *dead*? It seemed impossible.

His mind jumped to their last meeting and hastily backtracked from that contentious recollection again. *Not* his most shining moment. His strong bone structure tensed with strain: he really didn't want to go there. It was well over a year since he'd had any contact with Oleia and he had had no idea that she had left London to make her home in the French capital. What on earth could Oleia have left him? She had no relatives, he recalled wryly. Orphaned as a child, Oleia had been raised by a godparent and she had gained full independence at eighteen once she'd come into a very extensive fortune left to her by her parents. He would fly over to Paris first thing the following morning, sort it out and be home again by evening without Tally being any the wiser.

Yet, avoiding any issue and employing secrecy went

against his inherently forthright nature. But the desire to keep his wife happy was making Sander cautious and, for the first time in his life, keen to avoid potential sources of conflict. He had never liked surprises and it still bothered him that he had absolutely no idea why Tally had suddenly changed her mind and decided to give their marriage a second chance, for she was not a capricious personality. Now Oleia, who had never surprised him before this, he acknowledged. Perhaps the young Greek woman had left him some ironic gift as a footnote to their troubled relationship...and his lack of forgiveness. Sander was very conscious at that moment that he had never found it within himself to forgive Oleia for sleeping with another guy when they were teenagers. Like the elephant who never forgot, he had retained a grudge and in retrospect that struck him as a sad indictment of his male ego. Had Oleia had to die for him to appreciate how senseless it had been to nourish a grievance for so long?

The next morning Sander did not expect Tally to wake up before he departed for his early flight to Paris. He was in the kitchen nursing a cup of black coffee when she appeared in the doorway. Wrapped in a fluffy pink robe, she looked incredibly cuddly. Her green eyes were drowsy and her soft full mouth took on a tender curve as she surveyed him. 'So, you're still staging crack-of-dawn starts,' she reproved.

'*Because* I have an early flight and I want to be home for dinner.'

'Where are you off to?' Tally queried, her gaze

lingering on his lean devastatingly handsome features with helpless appreciation.

'Paris.'

Tally recognised the tension etched in the taut angle of his stunning cheekbones and the tightening round the corners of his wide, sensual mouth and wondered at it. 'Is there something wrong?'

Sander shrugged a broad shoulder. 'Why would there be?'

'Did you and your father have a disagreement recently?' she asked, suspecting that that might lie at the root of his tension. Sander was usually too loyal to complain about the problems he had with the older man.

Sander sighed. 'He's gone into virtual semi-retirement. He's never forgiven me for winning that vote of confidence from the board of directors.'

'You had to have their support to push through changes. He'll get over it.'

'Neither of my parents has a good track record for moving on,' Sander reminded her wryly.

And that was a truth and no mistake, Tally conceded ruefully when Sander had gone. Even when she was carrying their unborn grandchild, Petros and Eirene Volakis had made no attempt to welcome her into the family circle. They had kept her at arm's length in much the same way as they treated Sander. He was their son but forever doomed to live in the shadow of his late brother, Titos, who had died in a car accident a few years earlier. Their attitude infuriated Tally, who knew that it had been Sander who had saved Volakis Shipping after Titos had steered the family firm to the edge of destruction.

While Sander was in Paris, Tally was looking forward to a relatively laid-back day browsing through furniture showrooms on behalf of a client. Sander caught his flight and had to wait for his appointment at Edouard Arpin's offices. That waste of time chafed his already stretched nerves. When he was finally ushered into the solicitor's room only to be handed a handwritten letter, which he was assured would answer his questions, he was far from impressed.

It was a letter from Oleia and, apparently, a long-winded one.

'This is crazy.' Gritting his even, white teeth, Sander shook out the sheets of closely written notepaper with an air of long-suffering male incomprehension. Why the hell would Oleia have chosen to write him a letter? Who on earth wrote letters these days?

'I believe everything will be clearer once you have read my late client's explanation,' the solicitor remarked as he left Sander alone in the room.

Suppressing a groan of exasperation and extending his long powerful legs in an attitude of resolute relaxation, Sander settled down to read.

Unfortunately he hit a rock that derailed him at the same instant that he came on the unexpected word, 'baby'. Frowning in bewilderment, because he had no idea where the reference to an infant had sprung from, he had to retrace several lines and read with greater care and concentration. As he read an awful presentiment of impending doom began to creep through his big powerful length like spooky fingers of frost. His worst expectations fulfilled, he sprang upright in a sudden movement of repudiation with a curse on his lips and flung the letter violently aside.

No, it *couldn't* be true, he reasoned in thundering disbelief, unable to read any further because acting the role of passive victim made him feel like a rat caught in a trap. He could *not* have got Oleia pregnant when he had briefly turned to her for consolation after his marriage had disintegrated... Could he have? Hypothetically speaking, he was grudgingly forced to admit that as his recollections were vague in the extreme such a development was humanly possible.

But surely God would not punish him that harshly? Had he not already lost a child? Sander clung to the comforting belief that he had paid his dues with pained conviction. He refused to credit that one ill-conceived night with the wrong woman could serve him with so brutal a retribution as a baby, a consequence that his wife would never accept or forgive. He had made a mistake and he had known as soon as he made it. He had also immediately done what he could to redress the balance with honesty. Even so, that night had lain on his conscience ever since.

And only now was he learning—too late to change anything—that Oleia had fallen pregnant that same night and had chosen to keep the fact a secret from him. She had duly given birth to a little girl—but what the heck had she done with the child? Breathing audibly from lungs that felt constricted and with a fine veil of perspiration now forming on his brow, Sander was forced to retrieve the letter and read on a good deal faster than he had previously done to answer that all-important question.

Apparently, Oleia had called her daughter Lili and she had not put the child up for immediate adoption as he might have assumed. It was even more of a challenge for him to imagine a free-spirited party girl like Oleia willingly assuming the responsibilities of a single parent. In fact he could not imagine that miraculous development at all. Yet evidently that, and in his opinion inconceivably, was what Oleia had done.

Making it clear that she had long foreseen his likely reaction to the sudden shocking news that he was a father, Oleia had informed him in her letter that she had left a sample of Lili's hair with a reputable French DNA testing agency so that Sander could have a test done and check out the child's parentage for his own satisfaction. There was something so frighteningly factual about that obliging information that it punched a substantial hole in the barrier of Sander's disbelief. He folded the letter and dug it into a pocket, unable to face reading any further revelations before he had come to terms with what he had just learned. Could it be true that he had become a father without knowing it? That he had fathered a child with Oleia Telis? Shock and consternation ripped through Sander like a paralysing electrical current and it was at that juncture, while he was frozen by the window with preoccupied eyes, that Edouard Arpin chose to rejoin him.

The lawyer spoke clearly and concisely and Sander finally understood why his presence had been so urgently required in Paris. A four-month-old little girl had just lost her mother and now Sander was her legal guardian. Whether or not he felt the need to check out Lili's exact parentage was Sander's own private business and had no bearing on the reality that, regardless of what he discovered in that line, he would still be officially responsible for the welfare of Oleia's daughter.

When he questioned Edouard more closely about the circumstances of Oleia's death he was dismayed to be told that Oleia's party lifestyle had probably weakened her immune system and led to the pneumonia that had killed her. In addition Lili's current living arrangements could not continue as her nanny had already handed in her notice. Decisions had to be made and quickly.

As a guy who had already paid a steep price for his unwillingness to commit to the responsibility of being a parent, Sander felt as if he were walking on eggshells over ground he had hoped he'd never have to cover again. In the back of his mind he could not help but ask himself what Tally would expect from him. He knew that his reluctance to be a father had caused the first cracks in his marriage and had further contributed to Tally's lack of faith in him as a husband. After all, Tally had had a hopeless father figure in Anatole Karydas, which had ensured that she set a very high value on a man's ability to be a good parent. He could only wish that that painful truth had occurred to him when they were first married.

Within ten minutes of leaving Edouard Arpin's office, Sander was on the way to the DNA testing agency, keen to get that formality settled and out of the way.

The procedure, the taking of a saliva swab, took only seconds. At Oleia's apartment, Sander was greeted by the nanny, Suzette, a thin, frowning blonde, and before he even got as far as the hall he received a stream of complaints.

Her charge was *impossible*…refused to sleep…eat… stop scratching. How soon would the new nanny be arriving? In the background a baby was wailing incessantly. It was shrill, forlorn crying and an assault on Sander's eardrums. His brow furrowing, a pained look in his dark eyes, he admitted that he had yet to hire a replacement nanny but that he would be doing so immediately. He offered to significantly increase Suzette's salary if she would stay on until he could put other arrangements in place. A smile removing the sour slant from her lips, the blonde agreed and insisted on showing him straight into the nursery.

So great was the noise that Sander would not have been surprised to see an entire row of screaming babies in the room, but the big centrally placed cot contained only one very small child. It had to be said that Lili was a very miserable-looking baby. Her very red face was screwed up unattractively and swollen, her equally undersized limbs lost and flailing around in the folds of a baby suit that was too large. No magical sense of recognition or bonding assailed Sander, who had to work hard just to stand his ground in spite of the appalling racket.

For an instant he recalled on a sharp surge of grief the baby son who had failed to even draw breath at birth. He remembered those terrible minutes while the doctors had worked frantically in an effort to save the life already lost. He remembered that hideous silence, when any sound from their son would have been welcomed, finally being torn apart by Tally's sobs of disbelief. He remembered trying to be strong for her, which basically had meant not crying alongside her while he wondered insanely if his lukewarm attitude to becoming a father could have somehow caused the tragedy.

'Does Lili often cry like this?' he enquired without any expression at all.

'*Toujours*…always,' the nanny contended wearily. 'I get no sleep.'

Unable to summon up at will a more acceptable emotional response, Sander strove to be practical instead. He questioned the nanny carefully about Lili's short life to date and his lean strong face took on a grave aspect. The baby would have to be taken to London. The Paris apartment would be cleared and the contents stored until someone had time to go through them and see if anything ought to be kept. Returning to the hall, which was at least quieter, Sander called his PA in London and then Edouard Arpin and did what came naturally to him: he made arrangements and reached decisions. He contacted an agency in London and was promised the crème de la crème of nannies to care for Lili in the hotel suite he had booked for her occupation. He saw no space for inspiration in any of the choices he made. To look after Lili he had to take her back to London with him and he could scarcely take her home to Tally. His brain found it impossible to move beyond that boundary.

'I will travel to London with her and pass her over to the new nanny,' Suzette conceded reluctantly.

By that stage, Lili had cried herself to sleep. Sander gazed broodingly down at the slumbering child. He saw no familiar Volakis traits in her indistinct features and felt absolutely nothing. Was this wretched little waif his daughter? His flesh and blood? His conscience was pricked and he was angry with himself. Shouldn't he feel *something*? Or was it shock freezing his responses? He had one final act to perform in Paris: he bought the orchids Oleia had loved, flaunting blooms in her favourite scarlet, and set them on her grave. For the first time he wished he had some of Tally's faith but he could find no comfort in prayers. What had happened had happened, and nothing he said or felt in retrospect could change that hard fact.

When Sander phoned that evening to say he wouldn't be back until the next day instead, Tally was not that surprised. He sounded preoccupied and she assumed his mind was still on business. But just thirty minutes later she received another call, which took her very much by surprise. That second call came from her half-sister, Cosima Karydas, and it broke a silence that had lasted for well over two years, during which time Cosima had ignored Tally's wedding in order to maintain her distance from her illegitimate elder sibling. Cosima, Anatole's younger daughter, born of his marriage to a Greek woman, had never really come to terms with the existence of Tally, who had been raised apart from Cosima and with none of the material advantages Cosima took for granted.

'My goodness, Cosima…' Tally exclaimed.

'Sorry I haven't been in touch…you know how it is when you're busy—'

'Of course I do,' Tally responded, relieved to hear from the younger woman again.

'Would you be free for lunch tomorrow? I'm dying to see you!'

Pleased by Cosima's enthusiasm but wryly amused at her impatience after so long a silence, Tally mentally rescheduled an appointment and agreed to meet up. Her sibling made a predictably late arrival. Heads turned to follow Cosima's enviably shapely figure as she crossed the restaurant. With silky dark wings of hair framing her bright dark eyes she was very pretty girl.

'I gather you're back with Sander,' Cosima remarked over a glass of wine. 'I don't blame you: he's gorgeous.'

Tally went pink and smiled, heartened by her sister's easy acceptance of their reconciliation. 'He still floats my boat.'

'Boat… Volakis Shipping… Pun! Well, it's good to know you haven't lost your sense of humour.' In spite of that sentiment, however, the younger woman still looked very tense. 'I've heard something. I just had to check it out with you, though you'll have to promise first not to tell Dad that I passed it on…'

Tally's smooth brow furrowed. 'I won't repeat anything you tell me.'

'You weren't always so scrupulous,' the younger woman reminded her ruefully.

Tally took that on the chin, for she had once reported

Cosima's wrongdoing to their father to ensure that *she* did not carry the can for things that had gone wrong while both were staying for a weekend at a country house. 'You were much younger then.'

Cosima winced. 'And in the wrong when I spiked your drink at that party,' she slotted in, shamefaced. 'I'm sorry about that and sorry, too, I didn't have the guts to apologise at the time.'

'It's over and done with,' Tally said soothingly.

Cosima rested troubled eyes on Tally. 'You're making me feel awful. I just can't tell you the story I heard recently…'

'I haven't a clue what you're talking about—'

'I know and that makes it worse,' Cosima complained.

'Start at the beginning,' Tally advised. 'That's usually the best place.'

'Once upon a time,' Cosima began in a teasing tone but her eyes were troubled and evasive, 'there was a very beautiful girl called Oleia…Oleia Telis.'

Every scrap of colour slowly drained from Tally's cheeks, her eyes reflecting the jolt of shock she had received at hearing that particular name spoken out loud for the first time in a very long time. 'I've heard about her.'

'So you know that Oleia and Sander—'

'Were an item when they were teenagers,' Tally slotted in flatly, wondering why her sibling was subjecting her to such an unwelcome reminder.

'A little bird in Athens is suggesting that they've been together a lot more recently than that,' Cosima let drop in a concerned undertone. 'I thought you should know. I honestly didn't want to upset you. I just thought you shouldn't be left in the dark while other people talk behind your back.'

Tally grimaced at that frank admission. 'I'm not in the dark. I met Oleia once and it was a memorable occasion. There's not much she wouldn't do to get Sander back, so I'm not surprised there's gossip doing the rounds.'

'This is more serious than gossip. There's a rumour that there's a child,' Cosima almost whispered.

'A child?' Tally gave her pretty sibling an arrested look and her eyes widened with disbelief. 'Sander and Oleia's? That's *outrageous*. Of course there isn't a child!'

'If you're sure.'

There was an angry sparkle now in Tally's green eyes. 'Of course I'm sure. Where did you hear this ridiculous rumour?'

'I heard my father discussing it with my mother. Before you ask, he had no idea whether it was true or not and I was forbidden from mentioning it to you or anyone else,' Cosima confided with a grimace. 'He was furious I'd overheard their conversation.'

Renewed shock had made Tally's heartbeat thud so loudly in her ears that she thought it might stop dead and never start again. The reference to Anatole, whom she knew to be a fertile source of all kinds of confidential information in Greek society, disturbed her. Naturally she had no very clear idea of what Sander had been doing during their separation, but she was convinced that an ambition to father a child with Oleia

Telis would not have featured. Nor, considering his feelings for his one-time girlfriend, could she credit that he would have chosen to get involved with the glamorous brunette again.

In fact, self-evidently, Cosima was repeating a nasty, malicious rumour and Tally considered herself to be too sensible to pay heed to that sort of nonsense. Someone knew about Oleia's obsession with Sander and had spitefully put that together with the fact that Sander's first child had been stillborn. What other connection could there be? She did not think she had ever heard a more unpleasant piece of gossip!

'I just thought that if it was me in your position, I'd want to know,' Cosima told her silent companion awkwardly in the humming silence. 'Oh, Tally, should I have kept quiet?'

Tally assured her half-sister that it was only a silly story and not worth getting upset about. She hoped the hollow note in her own voice was not recognisable. Keen to seem impervious to what she had been told, she remarked on how hungry she was and ordered a snack for lunch, only to push it round the plate, praying that Cosima was too intent talking about her latest boyfriend to notice that Tally had mislaid her supposedly healthy appetite.

Obviously the reference to a child was manufactured twaddle to add drama to the scandals that had once dogged Sander's every footstep as a single man. All the same, Tally reasoned, it was not unlikely that Sander might have met up with the beautiful Greek girl again and not impossible that the attraction between them could have revived. Her glass held like a shield in a white-knuckled grip, Tally sipped her wine and thought and fretted about Sander, whom she loved with an all-consuming passion that sometimes scared her...

Sander, who often did the unexpected and whose thoughts and actions she could never second-guess. Sander, who could be as volatile as petrol sprayed on a blazing fire...

# CHAPTER SIX

ON THE flight back to London on his private jet, Sander was served with a tasty early dinner. He felt like the condemned man being presented with a last meal and eventually nudged the plate away untouched.

Lili was an unforgettable presence because she cried throughout the flight. The combined attentions of her nanny and the cabin crew made no impression on her and the playful sallies and compliments the baby attracted soon dried up. Regardless of whether she was held, rocked or fed, Lili sobbed inconsolably. Sander decided the child needed a doctor to check her over and possibly a nanny with a more nurturing approach. Lili had not inherited her mother's cute factor and her incessant crying and seeming unresponsiveness to her handlers would have taxed the patience of even the keenest carer. But it was first and foremost *his* job to look out for her needs, he recognised grimly.

*Tally would never forgive him.*

The thought sliced like a rapier through his brain, shooting him back on target to reality with a stinging jolt. Sander drew in a shuddering breath and bolted down another whisky without appreciating the flavour of its rare vintage. He had to tell Tally about Lili before someone else did because Lili's existence would unleash the kind of feverish speculation that the gossip columnists and, it had to be admitted, many of his friends revelled in. But how could he tell his wife that he had fathered a baby by another woman after their own child had died? It would be too cruel to tell her such a thing, yet to remain silent was equally impossible. No, he decided heavily, there was no escaping the inevitable and there *were* no adequate words to describe such a departure from good taste and acceptable behaviour.

Tally had made a conscious effort to get home early that afternoon in order to dress up for Sander's return. When she was a teenager she'd had a different attitude, deeming the urge to put on an artificial show for a man degrading. But she had learned to think differently while married, once she'd seen how a glimpse of sensual lingerie or a revealing outfit could light a fire in Sander's eyes that he couldn't control. It had given her a taste of feminine power that she liked very much. And, in the vicinity of a male who could leave her dry-mouthed and breathless with one winging glance, she had enjoyed that sense of equality.

Of course, lighting fires carried the obvious cost of extinguishing them again, she acknowledged with pink cheeks as she chose a dress made of a stretchy purple fabric that moulded the swell of her breasts and hips and slid her feet into velvet open-toed stilettos. Cosima's tale had seriously rattled the bars of the cage that held her insecurity. Tally could have done without the knowledge that a rapacious beauty like Oleia was out there ready to move in and take full advantage of Sander's relatively recent availability. Sander was a very attractive, very wealthy, man and the promises inherent in the wedding rings they had once worn had been damaged by their separation. This time around Tally felt that she could not afford to take anything for granted. It would take time and effort to build the bonds of trust again. And, in the short term, she could not take Sander out of circulation, she could only hope that he valued their marriage enough to respect it.

Sander knew exactly what he was going to say when he got home; well, he knew it right up until he walked into the bedroom where Tally, one stiletto heel braced on a chair, was straightening a gleaming silk stocking the colour of a freshwater pearl on a slender thigh. Stockings and suspenders really did it for him but she rarely wore them because she found them uncomfortable. The startling surge of response in his groin as he glimpsed the taut strip of fine fabric between her thighs sent his brain reeling into a plunge bath of sensual awareness that did nothing to sharpen his wits. He knew an invitation when he got one and he almost groaned out loud in his frustration because he knew he dared not touch her just then: but, conversely, he also knew he might never touch her again once he had finished telling her what she had to be told. The reflection threatened to tear him in two with rare indecision.

'Sander...I assumed you'd be later than this.'

As she met the stunning golden gaze welded to her with such explicit appreciation a hot ache stirred low in Tally's pelvis. Sander was watching her intently from the threshold of the room. With an impatient hand he thrust the door open wider, striding in and angling a hip back against the door to close it: a lean powerful figure in a designer suit with hard bronzed features and eyes full of predatory fire. Her Greek husband was all male and irresistible. His attention did not once waver from her and she trembled with pronounced awareness. He was so damn beautiful he made her skin tighten over her bones, her heartbeat thump like a panic alarm shrieking through her treacherous body. She understood why Oleia had never got over losing him and knew she intended to hang onto him, whatever it took.

'The jet got an earlier take-off slot…love the stockings,' Sander husked, coming to a halt and lifting the leg she had lowered to brace it back on the edge of the chair again. 'Loved the view of you standing there. Like my every fantasy brought to life even more, *yineka mou*.'

The brush of his fingertips against her thigh made her shiver. She stared up at him, raspberry tinted lips slightly parted, and he bent his handsome dark head and tasted her mouth with hungry driving brevity. It only made her want his mouth more and she lifted a hand to snare it in the springy depths of his black hair and draw him back to her again. He kissed her with devastating urgency while he trailed long brown fingers up the length of her raised leg, sliding below the hem of her dress and pushing it out of his path. Knowing that if she looked down she would see her knickers exposed, she felt shameless, but her body was pulsing on red alert. A fingertip skated over the most sensitive area of her entire body and she stopped breathing, time suspended as he lingered on the tiny cluster of nerve endings that controlled her. He released her mouth long enough for her to moan in response and watched her as she pushed against his teasing hand.

'I want you *so* much,' Sander admitted in a roughened undertone, tugging the thin band of silk away from her overheated flesh.

He cast off his jacket, wrenched loose his tie and dropped down on his knees. She made a muffled sound of protest, which he ignored as he trailed down her knickers with determined hands. The first brush of his tongue at the moist heart of her sent a violent shiver of response through her and he closed supportive hands to the backs of her thighs, gently but firmly easing her back against the bed until she folded down backwards on it.

Tally lay back, legs spread, feeling wanton, her hands clutching into the bedspread below her fingers. Sander teased her with his mouth and tongue and a kind of strangled gasp escaped her, arousal shoving surge after surge of heat through her trembling length. Her body went out of control incredibly fast and she hit a shattering climax that roared through her like a tornado.

Seconds later, Sander sank into her still frantically aroused body and she could not resist the hunger he reignited. She was conscious of her intense pleasure when he reached the same completion in the circle of her arms. Afterwards she lay against him listening to the solid reassuring thump of his heart beneath her cheek while her limp body still hummed from a surfeit of excitement.

'The only really sensible thing I ever did in my life was marry you,' Sander muttered shakily, his broad chest heaving as he struggled to catch his breath again.

'And even then my father had to twist your arm to get you to the altar,' Tally could not resist reminding him.

Brilliant dark eyes welded to her flushed face, Sander closed his arms round her in a crushing embrace and pressed his mouth to her smooth brow in a soothing benediction. Marmalade strands of hair tickled his chin. 'He didn't do *you* a favour, *yineka mou.*'

A little surprised by that uncharacteristic burst of self-mockery, Tally luxuriated in his affection and wrapped her arms round him.

Sander released her to sit up. 'I need a shower.'

Closing his bleak gaze, he sprang off the bed without further ado to head into the bathroom. Reality had reasserted its cruel hold on him. When he reappeared still towelling himself dry, Tally was dozing and he leant down to shake her awake.

'What?'

'Get dressed. We need to talk about stuff…you and I,' he extended flatly.

The rarity of such an announcement from Sander, who never talked about anything relationship-orientated if he could avoid it, sent Tally's sleepy eyes flying back open. She pushed up on an elbow and frowned at him. *'Talk?'*

Sander nodded silently as though he had already used up his entire allotted vocabulary for the day. His lean strong face was taut and grim, his handsome mouth compressed.

A chill ran through Tally. 'Something's wrong,' she guessed.

'I probably shouldn't have taken you to bed,' Sander conceded, a line of dark colour accentuating the stunning slant of his cheekbones. 'But I couldn't resist the temptation.'

Tally, engaged in peeling off the stockings, which, now they'd worked their magic, she was keen to dispense with, shot him a troubled glance. 'Is this serious?'

His gaze avoided hers and she could see that he was paler than usual below his golden skin tone. 'Very. I'll wait for you downstairs.'

Tally had the fastest shower on record while she ran through all the possible bad things that could have happened to bring that austere aspect to her husband's handsome dark face. Sander was usually bombproof, untouched by the colossal insecurities that afflicted other less confident personalities, so she discarded the idea that he might be exaggerating the situation. Could it be a business disaster? Business was the most important element in Sander's world and if anything went wrong he would regard it as a personal failing, which he would feel duty bound to confess. A major row with his father? A necessary parting of the ways?

If he had had to leave Volakis Shipping, he would undoubtedly have to rethink his financial outgoings, she reflected ruefully—her pensive gaze scanning the undeniable luxury of her surroundings. Sander had considerable pride, and retrenchment would strike him as humiliation. But Tally, raised by a mother whose finances were meagre, invariably unreliable and built on false hopes, was unconcerned by the prospect of a less indulgent lifestyle. But then Tally had considered herself to be comfortably off when she could simply pay her bills without having to follow a strict budget.

In the drawing room, Sander realised that he wanted another drink and he resisted the urge. Right now that was not the support he needed. He was painfully aware that the amount of alcohol he had consumed during his flight home had already dangerously clouded his judgement. How else could he explain the scene he had instigated in the bedroom? He should have restrained himself. His lack of control and foresight shocked him. He was convinced that he had made an already bad situation worse.

As relaxed as her husband was tense, Tally strolled in. She still looked deliciously tousled and flushed from their lovemaking and the figure-hugging purple dress looked stupendously sexy on her shapely curves. Her green eyes were sparkling. Regret cut through Sander like winter ice, burning and cutting wherever it touched because he knew that the warmth he had rekindled in Morocco would be killed by what he had to tell her.

'I have a confession to make,' Sander breathed starkly, ready to plunge straight in at the deep end.

Tally's happy conviction that nothing she really needed to worry about was amiss took a beating at that moment with Sander poised in front of her as though he were facing a firing squad. Raw tension vibrated from every lean-muscled inch of his tall powerful physique. 'I didn't think you did confessions,' she muttered uncertainly, 'and I'm not sure they're always a good idea.'

'Soon after we broke up, I slept with Oleia Telis,' Sander admitted stonily.

Tally received that admission as though she had been punched when she least expected it. Strive though she did to seem strong and untouched, she flinched and the colour drained from her cheeks. Cosima's story had made her wonder on the basis that there was rarely smoke without fire. But she would have very much preferred to have been left wondering. It would have been more bearable, she reflected dully, to be left ignorant of what might have taken place between Sander and the young woman he had loved and given up as a teenager.

Tally could not help picturing the tiny, fairy-like brunette in her mind's eye. Unfortunately, Oleia Telis possessed that lethal brand of intense femininity and flawless beauty that would always turn male heads. At the very thought of Sander in bed with Oleia nausea rippled through Tally's tummy. Her imagination did not want to go there and her thoughts refused. Even so, a mindlessly ferocious wave of bitter hurt was speedily engulfing her. Of all the women Sander could have turned to, why had he had to choose Oleia? The very woman Tally felt she could least overlook. She knew enough about Sander's perverse relationship with Oleia to be convinced that anything he had shared with Oleia would not have been either meaningless or forgettable.

'I ran into her at a party here in London. We have… *had*…so many mutual friends,' Sander advanced with reluctant precision. 'It was a one-night stand, Tally. A mistake on my part—'

'A...*mistake*,' Tally echoed with an unintentionally jagged laugh of disagreement at that choice of word.

'One I very much regret,' Sander continued curtly. 'She was the last woman I should have got involved with.'

Green eyes, sharp as knives, collided with his. 'So, why did you?'

Sander knew exactly what had driven him into Oleia's arms. It was actually very simple. But he did not think at that moment there was any point in sharing his reasoning, which had, admittedly, been of the very basic masculine variety. He felt he had said enough about that night and that to say more with regard to the detail lent the issue too much importance.

'When you walked out on me in France, the whole frame of my life was based on our marriage, on my being a married man, a husband. Without that frame I felt...*strange*.' The word was voiced with a grimace of discomfiture. 'I needed company and distraction and I was drinking a lot...I was on a bender the weekend I ran into Oleia,' he confided in a driven undertone, the words ricocheting from him like a volley of bullets. 'I hardly remember anything about that night.'

'That's convenient,' Tally remarked flatly, struggling not to think of him blundering around drunk and vulnerable within reach of Oleia's cunning, calculating little claws. It made her feel unduly and distressingly responsible; as if she had handed her husband over to the other woman, who'd long wanted him back on a plate.

Sander sent her a level glance. 'You may see it as convenient but it also happens to be the truth.'

'Before we got married you told me that you'd never get involved with Oleia again, that you couldn't forgive her for sleeping with someone else when you were dating as teenagers,' Tally reminded him curtly. 'So, naturally, I'm surprised that you should've ended up with her again.'

'It was wrong from every angle but I couldn't see that until the next day when I was sober enough to realise what I had done. Oleia was aware that our marriage had broken up and was…understandably, I suppose…hoping for more than I was willing to offer.'

'Nice to be so much in demand,' Tally commented brittly, her chest tight with pain, since he was reminding her why she had most feared Oleia Telis as a rival. It was true that Oleia had betrayed Sander by sleeping with someone else. But, surprising though it might seem in the circumstances, it also did look as though Oleia had actually loved Sander. After all, the brunette had regretted her behaviour to the extent that even years after the event she had still been set on getting Sander back.

'No, a humbling experience,' Sander traded flatly, his darkly handsome features shuttered. 'Whatever I was going through at the time I should have left her out of it.'

Evidently, he had slept with Oleia and walked away again, feeling guilty that he did not have more to give his former girlfriend. So, it could only have been sex or the combustible combination of alcohol and sex that had powered their reunion. The very thought of such intimacy between them still hurt though. Teeny tiny Oleia had finally got her wish and got Sander back, however briefly the liaison had lasted. Was she to believe that the liaison had proved brief?

'And I'm afraid that the repercussions from my blunder didn't end there,' Sander gritted, stunning dark eyes fixed to Tally with an intensity she could feel, his lean strong face clenched hard with strain. 'Oleia apparently fell pregnant and gave birth to a child a few months ago.'

An unearthly silence greeted that announcement.

Gooseflesh bloomed on every inch of skin exposed by Tally's dress. Shock was slamming hard through her and reducing her to the limp equivalent of a crash dummy. She parted pale bloodless lips and studied him as if she was still struggling to make what he had said comprehensible. 'That's not possible.'

'I wish it hadn't been but it seems that it was. I took a DNA test yesterday in Paris,' Sander revealed, employing a level of detail that impressed her as far too realistic to feature in what she had hoped was a crazy misunderstanding.

'A baby?' Tally whispered sickly, sweat breaking out on her short upper lip because her body was weak and reeling and a horrible light headedness was attacking her. 'You've had a baby with Oleia Telis?'

His heavily lashed dark eyes flared vibrant gold as the sun. 'Do you think I wanted this to happen? Choice had nothing to do with it!'

# CHAPTER SEVEN

TALLY had read about people hyperventilating and had often wondered exactly what it entailed. Now she was finding out in person. Her head was thumping and because she couldn't seem to get air into her oxygen-starved lungs she took faster, deeper breaths. But it didn't help because the dizziness and the tightness in her chest merely increased. In fear that she might faint and betray weakness, she rushed out of the room, paying no heed at all when Sander called her name in her wake.

Her heart thundering, her breath bursting noisily from her lips, she lurched into the cloakroom and flung herself back against the door staring at her reflection in the mirror. Her eyes looked like two dark holes in her pale face. Shock was still trammelling through her in sickening waves. She wanted to scream. Indeed an anguished scream was trapped in her throat, a scream of raging disbelief, pain and frustration.

How could fate be so vicious to her? Another woman had given birth successfully to Sander's child, while *her* baby had died. She couldn't handle that. She would never be able to handle it. It hurt too much to even think about it and she had not been able to think about it in his presence. A baby. He had had a living, breathing child with Oleia Telis! A surge of nausea forced Tally over to the toilet bowl where she lost her last meal. She wished she could get rid of her tormented thoughts as easily.

As she freshened up at the vanity unit stinging tears were running down her face and a savage sense of disbelief cut through her like a knife twisting slowly inside her. She was remembering her little boy, perfect in form but dead at birth: let down by the pitiful failure of her body to support her pregnancy. Her placenta hadn't developed properly and because of that her baby had not received the oxygen and nutrients he'd needed to survive. There had been no symptoms, no medical warnings, apart from the absence of a heartbeat when she went into labour, soon followed by the still, silent arrival of the little baby she had nurtured in her body for nine months.

Tally had had no reason to suspect that anything might go wrong. But she had still blamed herself, despising her body for letting her down when she most needed it to do a proper job and protect her baby. The doctor had told her it wasn't her fault, that there was nothing she could have done differently. He had also promised her that if she ever got pregnant again her condition would be carefully monitored to ensure the safe arrival of her child.

But in the meantime, it seemed that some other woman had borne that child for Sander. The stillbirth of their son had broken Tally's heart into jagged pieces. When she had emerged from hospital bereft, everything else in her world had become meaningless. Her husband? Her marriage? Nothing had mattered to her in the slightest while her empty arms simply craved the child she had lost. Seeing other people's babies had hurt so badly that she had not known how she could bear it. The hole in her life had been child-shaped and only her son could have filled it. Haunted by images of her little boy, for a while she had continually heard his phantom cries in nightmares when she would dream that he was lost and she would run around a bewildering maze of rooms frantically trying to find him. Night after night she had dreamt of such horrors and her need to avoid sharing those tormenting images with Sander had first led to her moving out of their bedroom into a guest room. Her excuse had been that her restlessness was disturbing his rest. In truth she had struggled to cope with waking him up and withstanding questions she did not feel mentally strong enough to answer. At one stage she had honestly feared that she was losing her mind and she had wanted to hide the fact, ironically afraid that if he knew how crazy she was becoming he would leave her just as her baby had already left her.

And now, at a time when Tally had finally decided to try and conceive again, she'd learned that Sander had already had a child with Oleia Telis. The outrageous rumour that Cosima had warned her about had proved to be true—a nightmare truth. She could *not* live with it…

Sander knocked frantically on the door. 'Tally…let me in, *please*!'

'Go away!' Choking back the sobs that were building up, Tally slid down the back of the door onto the cold tiled floor. She braced clammy palms on the icy tiles in an attempt to regain control. She was shaking all over and her very bones seemed to hurt. It was grief and because it was an old friend she recognised it: while sorrowing for her stillborn son she had lived with misery as her closest companion for many months. Yet she had found her path out of that long dark tunnel, turned her back on despair and begun to live again. But...*now*?

How could Sander, whom she had loved so much, have had a baby with Oleia? Her small hands closed into angry fists, bitterness drenching her emotions like an acid bath even as she succeeded in holding back the tears that threatened to fall. Had she not suffered enough? Had he not hurt her enough when their marriage had fallen apart? Oleia and Sander *and their child*. It was a concept that tore Tally into shreds, a snapshot of the dream family she had hoped that she and Sander would build and which she had cherished in her heart. Now that future possibility had been stolen from her.

'Tally...are you okay?'

'Of course I'm not okay?' she blasted back through the barrier of the door. 'How could you think I would be?'

'Unlock the door,' Sander ordered.

And Tally did what he demanded only because she could not stand to let him believe that she was hiding from him or the bombshell he had delivered. Rigid control tightening her heart-shaped face, she walked out, every movement as stiff as a board because she was holding herself so taut that her very muscles ached as though she had taken a physical battering as well as a mental one.

Sander rested his hands lightly on her taut shoulders. 'Please don't shut me out—'

'Why would I? This is your problem, not mine,' she pronounced coldly and even while she maintained her composure she was screaming underneath that superficial show. He had a baby with Oleia. He had become a father with Oleia. In a sudden motion she sidestepped him and shook off his hands to head for the stairs.

'I realise you're very upset.'

'Is that why you dragged me off to bed when you first came home?' Tally slung at him in bitter condemnation, enraged by the recollection of how he had swept her up in passion barely thirty minutes before he made a revelation that would destroy her world. 'Did you think sex would comfort me? Or that it would make what you had to tell me any more palatable?'

'I don't know what I was thinking of, *yineka mou*.' Sander spread his hands in a fluid movement of frustration. 'I don't think I thought at all. I just wanted you. I'm sorry.'

'No, you're not…sorry, I mean,' she framed fiercely, stalking up the stairs because she could no longer bear to look at him. 'You could never be sorry enough to satisfy me!'

And it was true, she reasoned dully as she hurried into her bedroom. There was nothing he could do to make everything better. There was no magic route for him to follow to win her forgiveness. As she knew with her own father a child was a lifetime commitment and once the child existed it could not be ignored, regardless of how she felt or indeed Sander felt. He had a duty to his child. Also, whether she liked it or not, he had a duty to Oleia.

Tally pulled an overnight bag out of the dressing room. She didn't know where she was planning to go, only that she could not stay below the same roof as Sander feeling as she did.

Sander stopped dead in the doorway and stared fixedly at the bag before lifting shaken golden eyes to her set face. 'You can't leave—'

'I can do whatever I like. Just as you have done,' Tally traded and then her soft mouth curled.

'Do you honestly think I wanted this situation?' he asked in blunt appeal.

The faintest colour blossomed in her wan cheeks as she acknowledged the truth of that claim. No, he would not have sought such a development, particularly not when he wanted a second chance at their marriage. In fact, nothing could be more disastrous for the prospects of their reconciliation than his discovery that he had fathered a child by another woman, Tally conceded dully. Unfortunately, her intellectual acceptance of those facts did not make one iota of difference to how she felt.

She tilted her chin in challenge. 'It's still your fault that this has happened.'

Watching her stuff sundry garments into the overnight bag with bleak, dark eyes, Sander clenched his wide sensual mouth hard. 'I admit that. I'm not trying to make any excuses for myself.'

'I *can't* accept Oleia having your child,' Tally framed

with a bitterness she could not hide, which already felt like a creeping darkness spreading inside her, freezing out warmer, more human emotions and the ability to think without feelings getting involved. She hated the way she felt—so desperately confused, unhappy and at odds with everything—almost as much as she hated him for hurting her.

All emotion on rigid lockdown, Sander was most concerned with the fact that Tally, who had only just come back to him, appeared to be walking out on him again. He didn't know what to say. His clever mind was as infuriatingly blank as an unwritten page, a rare state of affairs that mocked his superficial self-control. He wanted to act like a caveman and rip the bag off her and lock it away, lock *her* away just to keep her in his house. But that would be madness and fortunately his brain knew it, so that while his hands clenched into powerful fists of restraint he neither said nor did anything. His seething sense of frustration threatened to choke him.

In the humming deafening silence, Tally decided that she would simply return to her apartment for the night. She would have liked a friend to talk to, but she thought Cosima was too young and inexperienced and she didn't want to drag her mother into what was happening in her marriage. Unhappily, she did not feel close enough to Crystal to feel that she could safely share her sense of devastation with the older woman. And Binkie, whom Tally would once have confided in, was too far away in her current live-in employment in Devon to offer any support.

'Is it a boy or a girl?' That question about Oleia's

child sprang from Tally's tongue before she was even properly aware that she could not resist the temptation to ask it.

'A little girl,' Sander supplied gruffly. 'I honestly didn't know about her until the day before yesterday, Tally. But now that I do know I have to take care of her.'

'Of course,' Tally agreed woodenly, knowing what she ought to say as a decent human being, even if it wasn't necessarily what she was feeling.

'Right now I'm trying to hire a top-flight nanny. The child's current French carer, Suzette, wants to leave but the agency nanny I'd arranged to meet us in London cried off at the last minute,' Sander informed her gravely. 'I'm still waiting on a replacement arriving.'

In the act of yanking a jacket off a hanger in the dressing room, Tally peered back into the bedroom in surprise. '*You* had to engage a nanny? How did it become your job to organise child care?'

And Sander realised belatedly what he had not yet explained and he released his breath in a slow measured hiss, his even white teeth gritting. In as few words as he could manage he told her about Edouard Arpin's phone call and what his trip to Paris had entailed.

'But Oleia was so young; how can she be dead? What happened to her? Did she die in childbirth?' Tally queried incredulously, knocked off balance by the startling news that the young Greek woman was no longer alive.

'No, of course not. Lili's four months old. The French nanny said that Oleia was drinking heavily. When she came down with the flu it turned into pneumonia and she passed away within twenty-four hours of being admitted to hospital,' he advanced grimly. 'That's all that I know.'

So, Sander had literally been left holding the baby, Tally registered in considerable confusion, unsure how she felt about what she had just learned. By the act of dying, Oleia had made Sander fully responsible for his own child. Presumably when she drew up her will Oleia either hadn't known that Sander was not the most enthusiastic guy around when it came to parenting or she hadn't cared. Or perhaps Oleia had had nobody else for the role, Tally conceded—dismayed by her own lack of charity. Were angry resentment and hurt turning her into a thoroughly nasty person?

'Where are you planning to go?' Sander demanded abruptly, his Greek accent razoring along the edge of his diction in a dangerous warning of his stormy mood.

'Back to my apartment—for tonight anyway. I just need to be on my own,' Tally said, grimacing at the defensive note she could hear in her own voice.

'I'll book into the hotel if you like and you can stay on here,' Sander proffered, dark eyes keenly welded to her troubled face.

'I'd prefer to stay in my apartment.' Tally lifted the bag to walk to the front door.

'I don't want you to leave....'

Reluctantly she turned to look at him again. His proud, dark head was held high, his classic bone structure taut as he stared back at her, willing her to listen. 'I can't stay right now,' she told him doggedly.

'I'll give you a lift, then.'

In the end it seemed easier just to let him drop her off. But the atmosphere inside the car was suffocatingly tense. Lili, Tally was thinking painfully, a little girl. Oleia, whose powers of attraction Tally had feared and resented, had gone and left a legacy. A precious legacy, Binkie would have called the baby, while reiterating that every child was a gift from God and should be treated as such. How could she hate an innocent child, who had already lost her mother at such a young age? What had happened to her sense of compassion?

In the leather-scented comfort of the sleek Ferrari, Tally stole a glance at Sander, her attention lingering on his strong profile and the sweep of the ridiculously long lashes that shadowed his superb cheekbones. His gaze, deep-set and dark as pitch, swivelled and struck hers. As if she had been burned she dropped her eyes instead to the shapely male hands controlling the steering wheel. Only an hour ago those long brown fingers had stroked her body to ecstasy. Her face burned in mortification at the memory and somewhere in the region of her pelvis her body clenched tightly in on itself.

'You shouldn't be alone this evening,' Sander asserted.

'It's better than being with you,' she mumbled sickly, affronted by the way her thoughts were leaping and darting in all directions without an ounce of self-control.

'I shouldn't have made love to you,' Sander admitted in a dark driven undertone. 'But it wasn't calculated. I just couldn't resist you.'

'Like you couldn't resist *her*?' And the instant that

scornful comment escaped Tally she wished the words would disappear. She gritted her teeth together as if she was striving to physically restrain herself from asking anything else that might reveal the humiliating thoughts tormenting her.

Oleia was dead, but that didn't lessen the sense of betrayal Tally was experiencing. Once Oleia had basked in Sander's love. Love was a much deeper and more lasting emotion than Tally herself had ever stirred in her husband. That comparison could only wound. Sander had enjoyed Tally's company and had labelled her terrific in bed, but that had been the extent of her pulling power. Pain was steadily eating her alive and, just then, the prospect of Oleia's infant daughter was more than Tally could handle even thinking about. She thrust the knowledge of the child's existence deep, where it couldn't touch her. She wanted to forget. She wished he hadn't had to tell her: she wasn't a bad person, she was just human and weak, she told herself wretchedly.

Outside her apartment block, Sander sprang out and removed her bag from the car.

Across the low slung bonnet Tally clashed unwarily with his stunning dark golden gaze. It was one of those moments when Sander was unmistakeably CEO of Volakis Shipping, an international tycoon of considerable wealth and influence. He stood tall and straight, power etched in every masculine angle of his lean dark face.

'We have to deal with this as a couple. We still belong together, *yineka mou*,' Sander declared with admirable conviction as he reluctantly passed over the bag.

'Like oil and water?' Tally shot back at him, rage coming out of nowhere and surging up through her slim length like lava ready to overflow. Green eyes cutting as lasers, she glared at him. 'And don't call me *that*. Don't remind me that I'm your wife. It's hardly something I'm likely to boast about!'

Anger blazed hot as the sun in Sander's expressive eyes. 'Don't insult me. I have been as honest with you as I know how to be, but please don't forget that if you hadn't walked out on our marriage last year that child would never have been born!'

Cut to the bone by that bold reminder, Tally slammed the car door with violence. There was too much truth in that retaliation for her to brush it off and the last thing she needed to feel just then was that she had brought her sufferings down on herself. Outraged by his audacity, she stalked away without a backward glance. It was a relief to close the apartment door behind her and know that he could no longer witness her reactions, but she paced the confines of her home like a lost soul unable to find a place to settle. She knew she ought to eat but she wasn't hungry and when darkness fell she went to bed and prayed for sleep. Only sleep would give her solace, for at least while she slept she would not be forced to think any more.

Fate, however, still had one more punishment in store for her. Although it was a while since she had last had the nightmare in which she heard her son cry while she searched without success for him, she had a bad dream that night. A dream that ended with a different twist. In this new version she found the nursery where the baby was crying and rushed in, only to look down in horror into the cot at a totally unfamiliar child. That jarring experience woke her up with the sheet sticking to her perspiring skin. She was shaking so badly she could barely manage to switch the bedside light on. She had hoped those disturbing dreams, brought on by the grief that her mind was struggling to cope with, had gone for ever. The altered conclusion to the nightmare, clearly the result of what Sander had told her about his little daughter, Lili, was just one more slap in the face. She got up early and went for a shower, arriving at work well in advance of her staff.

Her mobile phone buzzed at eight-thirty. and she answered it. 'There's a story about Lili in the *Daily Globe* today,' Sander informed her grimly. 'Someone somewhere has talked out of turn. The paparazzi will be on your doorstep today looking for a reaction.'

Her strained face froze. 'I'll cope—'

'I don't think you should try. You should get out of London until the fuss dies down.'

'Nonsense. I have a business to run,' Tally fielded coldly, already in the act of searching on her computer for the online edition of the paper.

'I'm sending a security team over to your showroom. If you take my advice—'

'I won't,' Tally interrupted glacially.

'—you'll let them get you out of there before the proverbial hits the fan,' Sander murmured. 'With stories like this the paps can be very aggressive.'

'Then you should try not to lead the kind of life that

attracts them,' Tally retaliated sourly. 'Thankfully I *don't*—'

'It's just unfortunate that you married me,' Sander completed for her with sardonic bite.

She logged onto the newspaper's website and immediately saw the headline that screamed at her: *BILLION-POUND BABY!* Beside it was a picture of a very decorative blonde carrying a baby seat into a famous London hotel, Sander's tall, powerful figure recognisable several steps in her wake. The little girl's face was not visible. Her heart in her throat, Tally clicked on the item and began to read. Evidently Oleia Telis had died a hugely wealthy heiress and had left everything she possessed, including her child, to Sander, who was referred to as the 'hot-blooded Greek shipping magnate, currently pursuing reconciliation with his wife'. His relationship with Oleia was described as 'volatile but enduring' by a close friend who chose not to be named, the implication being that Oleia had become Sander's mistress during his marriage. That was an idea that had never occurred to Tally before and it knocked her for six.

Stunned, she suddenly felt the need for some fresh air and as she stumbled out of the entrance to her showroom a flash bulb went off and startled her into a standstill. As she glanced up in dismay a man demanded to know why she was no longer living with her husband. Aghast, Tally sped back into her office where her assistant, Belle, lifted her hand to grab Tally's attention and put the phone down saying anxiously, 'The phone has been ringing off the hook…the media asking nosy questions about—'

'I have no comment to make, no comment to make about anything,' Tally slotted in stiffly, her heart quickening its beat as another man strode in, a fancy camera dangled round his neck.

'I have some questions for Mrs Volakis,' he announced.

Tally straightened her slim shoulders but her colour was high. 'I'm not interested in answering questions. Please leave!'

But even as she spoke someone else was powering through the showroom door and asking loudly, 'Mrs. Volakis, did you know about your husband's baby by the Greek heiress, Oleia Telis?'

'Either you leave now or we call the police!' Belle threatened, standing her ground sturdily while the oafish young man attempted to push his way past her.

Something of a free-for-all was developing when the security presence that Sander had promised arrived in the persons of two, very large and powerfully built men who got rid of the obstreperous intruders with the minimum of commotion. By that stage, Tally had registered that there were now other paparazzi waiting out on the pavement and her earlier conviction that she could easily ride out any fuss was beginning to look naïve.

'I'm Johnson, Mrs Volakis. We'll take you out through the back entrance now.'

'I have an appointment—'

'I think you should take the day off,' Belle remarked with a grimace as yet another photographer rapped loudly on the window to get attention. 'If you're not here, they'll clear off.'

'I'm meeting Lady Margaret at ten—'

'I'll call and reschedule,' her assistant offered. 'I don't think she'd be too impressed if she had to wade through that scrum out there.'

Thinking of the very correct older woman, Tally was inclined to agree. While also thinking that such an un-savoury scandal would scarcely appeal to her clients and might indeed damage her business reputation. She lifted her bag and grabbed her coat to accompany the security men through the back entrance. As they tucked her into a big, black saloon car a man came running down the alley with a camera clutched in one hand. Her protectors threw themselves into the car and drove off at speed. Relieved to have escaped further harassment, Tally gave them her address.

'Your husband is expecting you to go to his new country house, Roxburn Manor,' Johnson imparted.

'I want to go to my own home,' Tally said firmly, while wondering when Sander had acquired the manor house. He certainly hadn't mentioned the fact to her. On some level it still shook her to be reminded that Sander had been leading an entirely separate life for many months and she could not understand why she should be reacting that way.

Exasperation gripped her when she saw a photogra-pher pacing outside her apartment building and the car had to accelerate away from the kerb again.

'We'll return to the original plan,' Johnson pro-nounced.

After her disturbed rest the night before, Tally was tired and in no mood to argue. She didn't want to go anywhere, she just wanted to vanish to a secluded place where she could feel safe from all the distressing elements currently infiltrating her world. Never had she felt as insecure as she did at that moment, she could not even take refuge in her apartment. Digging out her phone from her bag, she rang Sander.

'It's a two-day wonder, *glikia mou*,' he told her soothingly. 'It'll be someone else's turn to be worked over and chased round town next week. You'll get peace and quiet at Roxburn Manor.'

'All right, but just for a couple of days,' she agreed ruefully. 'I want to sleep for a week.'

'Are you sleeping properly?' Sander enquired in a tone of concern that she resented.

'I was sleeping perfectly until you came back into my life!' Tally fielded thinly.

Ten minutes later, Johnson escorted her into the lift of a skyscraper office block and up out onto the roof where a Volakis helicopter awaited them. Tally scrambled in and buckled up, only realising as she did so that she didn't even have a change of clothes with her. Just then her lack of luggage didn't seem that important: she was in a daze, almost traumatised by the fast-moving events of the past twenty-four hours.

The journey in the helicopter provided a welcome distraction from her unhappy thoughts. The sky hung blue and clear above a world composed of green fields and woods broken up by occasional settlements of small houses. Roxburn Manor, however, was a somewhat more impressive building, she registered as the helicopter came in to land within yards of a very elegant Georgian mansion. Mrs Jones, the housekeeper, greeted Tally with a warm smile and took her straight through the big airy hall into a spacious reception room where a log fire was burning in the grate to take the chill off the cool early summer day. A tray of refreshments arrived and lunch was discussed.

Tally had not realised quite how tired or how hungry she was until she sank into the opulent feathered comfort of a capacious sofa and let the tension fall away. A cup of tea and several biscuits later, she kicked off her shoes, curled up and sleep overtook her. It was dusk when she awoke. Darkness lay beyond the firelight flickering bright reflections on the windows and the noise that had wakened her was the sound of a helicopter landing. Her brow pleating she sat up, pushing her tumbled hair off her brow and searching for her shoes.

A light knock sounded on the ajar door and the house-keeper glanced in. 'Mrs Volakis? I didn't like to wake you for lunch but now that your husband's arrived, I'll ensure that dinner is served without delay.'

Wide awake now, Tally scrambled off the sofa, green eyes huge, mouth falling open in surprise. 'My husband?' she framed unevenly, unable to conceal her dismay.

Just then, she heard Sander's voice raised to address Mrs Jones and she stalked to the door in angry disbelief. What a fool she had been to blindly agree to being trans-ported to Roxburn Manor! Why hadn't it occurred to her that Sander might be planning to join her there? Or that Sander might use the harassment of the paparazzi as a weapon against her? Just when had she become so naïve that her astute husband could hoodwink her without effort?

Sander entered the hall, looking impossibly male, and tall and broad, in a dark cashmere overcoat worn over his business suit. Dark stubble roughening his strong jaw line, he turned hooded dark eyes on Tally's petite figure in the drawing-room doorway. 'Tally…Mrs Jones tells me you haven't eaten yet. I won't keep you waiting long—'

'I need to speak to you,' Tally began heatedly.

And then she heard a baby's unmistakeable wail somewhere nearby. Sander stepped to one side and a youthful brunette with a baby carrier appeared. Tally's attention homed straight in on the child it transported. Only part of a little red face and a quiff of curly dark hair showed above the edge of a rug. Paralysed to the spot by the sight, Tally lost every scrap of her angry colour and turned eyes of incredulous reproach on Sander before she wheeled round and retreated back into the drawing room, not trusting herself to speak while they had an audience.

Dear heaven, how could he set up such a confrontation? How could he bring that child to stay under the same roof as her? Did he have no conception of what he was doing to her? That was *his* child out there, the daughter he had had with Oleia! A soundless scream seemed to be stealing all the space in Tally's lungs and she knew that she was hyperventilating again…

# CHAPTER EIGHT

'TALLY…' Sander strode in and took off his coat, casting it down on a chair before closing the door to give them privacy.

Although Tally felt as though a large rock were sitting at the foot of her throat, she struggled to breathe normally again and loosen the choking tightness squeezing her chest. Sander focused deep-set eyes as tawny as a mountain cougar's on her rigid features. With faint colour scoring his strong cheekbones and accentuating the sleek angles and the hollows of his superb bone structure, he looked stunningly handsome and yet cautious as a man balancing on a rope above an abyss.

'How could you bring that child here?' Tally demanded starkly, her disbelief unhidden. At the same time she was resenting the undeniable buzz that his arrival evoked, the fizz in her bloodstream that acted like too much wine on a weak head. It mortified her that she could still be so aware of him.

'I couldn't just leave them in the hotel.'

'Why not?' Tally prompted, in no mood to be reasonable.

'Lili cries incessantly and she was disturbing the

other guests. The hotel management was complaining.' Sander compressed his wide sensual mouth as he made that exasperated admission. 'Suzette's replacement is new and inexperienced and she's struggling to cope. There's no way I could leave her in sole charge of Lili in London with a posse of paps hanging around looking for a photo opportunity.'

'All of a sudden you're acting so responsibly…like a *real* parent,' Tally sneered. She hated herself for doing it but could not swallow back the gibe.

'I'm doing my best,' Sander acknowledged curtly, his beautifully shaped mouth hardening on the acknowledgement. 'I have to: there's nobody else to do it.'

However, Sander's world was feeling like an ever-more hostile environment in which his every past sin came back to haunt him, many times. He was bleakly aware that he had not shone in adversity when Tally had fallen accidentally pregnant after they had been seeing each other for only a few weeks. The resentful edge of immaturity and the troubled childhood that had prevented him from accepting his new parenting role with enthusiasm had lingered with devastating results. He had kept his distance, preserving his detachment for the sake of his pride, and when the worst had happened it had proved too late in the day to turn the clock back and change anything.

Even through the solid thickness of the door Tally could hear the faint sound of the baby's heart-wrenching cries. Although the nanny had undoubtedly taken the child upstairs, she could still hear the little girl. Or was she simply *imagining* the fact that she could still hear the baby crying? Tally wondered worriedly. After all, she had already discovered that her imagination was boundless when sleep had plunged her back into the nightmares that had once haunted her. Her teeth gritted, her adrenalin jumping to sky-high levels at those cries, setting up a dim mocking echo in her ears. She wanted to run and keep on running but something steel hard inside her refused to give way to that craven urge. Any temptation to show weakness in Sander's vicinity had to be fought. Even if it killed her she would stay on at Roxburn Manor.

'I didn't even know *you* were planning to join me at this house, never mind bringing that child with you,' Tally condemned angrily. 'I'd never have agreed to leave London if I'd realised what awaited me here!'

Sander shifted a fluid brown hand as if to forestall that censure. 'I didn't think about that angle. I'm sorry. My only objective was to help you…'

'How can you help me? *You're my problem!*' Tally flung at him in a seething rage, glaring at him, her marmalade-coloured hair bouncing against her flushed cheekbones as she jerked an emphatic hand to underline that point. 'I wouldn't be running away from the press and their horrible nosy questions if it wasn't for you and your behaviour!'

Lean strong face clenched hard with self-discipline, Sander veiled his hot, golden gaze and squared his broad shoulders in resolute silence. He wanted to walk out, jump into the helicopter and go back to his office, where his best efforts invariably paid off with a profit. He was bloody marvellous at making money. He knew that, knew too that many women would regard it as his most appealing trait. For the first time he wished that diamonds were a currency that Tally appreciated. But when she had left a safe full of them behind when she'd walked out on their marriage, he had got the message that jewellery was no big deal for her. Tally expected more intangible and meaningful things from him. He just wasn't sure that he had whatever that was within him to give. And, unhappily, he didn't have the words to explain that lack to her either.

The smouldering silence of their mutual dissatisfaction was interrupted by the housekeeper inviting them through to the dining room for dinner Tally toyed with the idea of asking if she could eat upstairs in her room but she didn't want to act the demanding diva when she had no idea how much assistance the older woman might have in the household. Soft, full pink lips flattening with strain, she took a seat with an air of discomfiture in the stiflingly formal dining room.

'Why did you invite me here?' she asked after a young woman wearing an overall had served them with soup. 'If your arrival means that you think I'm accepting this situation—'

'Hardly,' Sander fielded that suggestion with a coolly raised ebony brow. 'I didn't want you struggling to cope with media intrusion when it was my fault that you had become a target. I thought you would get peace here.'

The soup was carrot and coriander and delicious. Tally wondered if it would warm the cold place inside her but reckoned that would take a blowtorch. 'When did you buy this house?'

'I *didn't*…buy it,' Sander tacked on when she looked back at him with a frown. 'Roxburn Manor belongs to my parents. About ten years ago my mother took the notion that she would like to live like an English country lady but one wet summer killed the dream. I can't recall when they last used this place.'

Tally studied the cool blue painted walls and highly ornate spindly furniture, which was so out of step with the age of the house, and thought that she should have recognised his mother's elaborate taste in interior design. With tact she made no comment about the wastefulness of retaining such a large property and not making use of it. She had never forgotten how very hard Sander had had to work to keep Volakis Shipping afloat while his parents continued to spend, spend, spend as though there were not a single cloud in their financial sky. Born into money, his parents were two of the most self-indulgent people she knew, yet Sander never ever criticised the extravagant lifestyle they took for granted. Considering the way his parents treated him, Tally saw his lack of complaint on that score as a phenomenon of filial loyalty and restraint.

Yes, Sander did have many good points, she acknowledged reluctantly. He was an excellent son to his undeserving parents, a hard worker, a terrific provider and a highly entertaining companion in and out of bed. But that thought process only sent Tally slap-bang, head first into a painful collision with the awareness of the one fact she could not surmount: Oleia's child. Tally's life had been turned upside down and there was nothing she could do about it, aside of walking away from

Sander and their marriage for good. Was that what she was planning to do?

Immobilised by the sheer threat of that prospect, Tally flinched when her mobile phone began to flash and buzz on the chair beside her.

'Leave it,' Sander told her impatiently.

Predictably Tally ignored that piece of advice and reached for the handset. It was Robert and an almost comical expression of dismay stamped her face.

'Where on earth are you?' he demanded. 'I've been waiting twenty minutes!'

Tally groaned out loud and began to apologise. The first Friday of every month, she and Robert always met over dinner to discuss business at her interiors firm and she had missed the previous month because she had been in Morocco. 'Robert, I am so sorry. I completely forgot that I was supposed to be seeing you tonight—'

'I can read newspapers,' Robert responded wryly. 'I know the rapturous reunion has to be hitting the skids fast under the tide of revelations coming out now in print.'

Her face flamed. 'Don't be sarcastic.'

'I'm very much on the outside with this, Tally,' her business partner said ruefully. 'I don't know what you expect from me.'

'Can't you just be my friend?' Tally questioned uncomfortably.

'You're making that a challenge. And blowing off Lady Margaret this morning wasn't a good move on your part. She's already been on the phone to complain to me. She doesn't want to be palmed off with one of your employees.'

Tally frowned. 'I assured her that any work she gives us would be receiving my personal attention. We were only going to have a preliminary meeting to discuss her preferences today.'

'Where are you?'

Outrageously conscious of Sander's hard questioning scrutiny, she explained about Roxburn Manor.

'I'll drive down and see you tomorrow around noon,' Robert told her and he cut off the call before she could protest.

Her strained eyes collided with Sander's steady dark golden gaze. *'What?'* she snapped in the uneasy silence that had spread.

'What's the state of play with Miller?' he queried in a charged undertone just as the woman in the overall reappeared to lift the plates and deliver the main course.

In the wake of her departure, Tally tilted her chin. 'My relationship with Robert is private.'

His intent gaze burned like the heart of a hot fire. 'Don't say that to me!'

'And don't push me to point out that what came out yesterday has forced me to reconsider our marriage!' Tally framed hoarsely, not wanting to make that threat but unable to silence the angry words brimming on her lips.

'I'm not stupid.' Sander studied her heart-shaped face, taking in the big green eyes torn by indecision and strain and the wounded curve of her luscious peach-tinted mouth. His appetite died there and then. He tossed his napkin down on the plate and vaulted upright. 'Excuse me: I also have a couple of calls to make.'

Tears stung Tally's eyes and she blinked them back angrily. She ate with dogged determination, recalling the many silent and lonely meals she had eaten when their marriage was falling apart in the South of France. While she'd been lost in grief, Sander had buried himself in work to the extent that she had felt alone and neglected and fully justified in deciding to leave him. But, just at that instant, she realised that maybe she had driven Sander away from her by reminding him that she no longer knew whether or not she was willing to give their marriage another go. She remembered her father's blackmail and almost laughed, knowing that he too would be watching events and wondering what the outcome would be.

History had repeated itself with the birth of an illegitimate child. Once she had been that child but at least she had been born *before* her father, Anatole, had met and married her half-sister, Cosima's, mother. Now she was getting a glimpse of what it felt like to be on the other side of the fence. She was full of angry resentment and uncharitable feelings for an innocent child who had not asked to be born. That acknowledgement only made Tally feel more wretched and confused than ever. It would probably be easier to walk away than to try and stay and make a go of their marriage in such circumstances, she reflected painfully. But the easier path wasn't necessarily the right one.

Mrs Jones showed her up to her room, her cheerful manner spelling out the reality that she was delighted that the manor was being occupied, even temporarily. In the background Tally tried not to listen to the mournful strain of Lili's continued howling from the floor above, while thinking that there surely had to be something amiss when a child cried so constantly and loudly and then hastily forcing the reflection back out of her mind again. A pile of boxes greeted her on the bed of the elegant guest room. Her investigations revealed a nightdress and wrap, as well as a skirt and sweater and lingerie all in the correct sizes. That was one thing about having a womaniser as a husband, Tally thought wryly, he really did know enough about her sex to understand what it took to make a woman comfortable.

But *was* Sander still a womaniser? Honesty bade her admit that she had had no reason to doubt his fidelity while they'd still been living together as man and wife. And he was right when it came to one major issue: she *had* abandoned their marriage. Only now did Tally recognise that grief had coloured everything she'd felt back then, adding to her unhappy conviction that her husband had only married her because she was pregnant. The stillbirth of their child had convinced her that there was no longer any reason for them to stay together and that Sander's constant absences were his way of telling her that. Now, recalling his admission that he had drunk heavily for a while after their break-up, she reckoned she was guilty of making too many assumptions—while ignoring the fact that Sander had always been bold enough to speak up on his own behalf.

Towelling herself dry after a quick shower, Tally put on the nightdress and wrap. All the while she was painfully conscious that Lili was still mournfully wailing at the top of the house. Finally she couldn't stand that muted sound in the background any longer and she stalked out of the room and headed off downstairs in search of Sander.

Sander was using his laptop at a vast and grandiose mahogany desk that was much more his father's style than his. When she appeared in the doorway, he glanced up with brilliant dark eyes and then visibly froze.

'To what do I owe the honour?' He savoured the sight of her in garments he had personally chosen for her. The costly turquoise silk lay in a fine glossy layer against her slight body, moulding the pouting curve of her breasts and the taut peaks. He hardened instantaneously, desire piercing his big powerful body with almost painful immediacy. The neckline of the wrap showed only a shallow vee of pale creamy flesh and yet that small glimpse of her velvet soft skin was the most erotic thing he had ever seen.

Beneath his steady scrutiny Tally reddened and stood rigid as a board. 'You probably won't think it's any of my business, but a baby that cries as much as Lili seems to—' she pronounced the name out loud for the first time and her voice faltered slightly over the word '—ought to be checked over by a doctor. Just in case she's crying because she's in pain…or something.'

Sander slid lithely upright, straightening to his full six-feet-plus height with fluid grace. Luxuriant black lashes semi-concealing his burning dark golden gaze, he sighed heavily. 'A doctor saw her in London. Apparently she suffers from infantile eczema and it's making her pretty miserable. The nanny has been given medication and a treatment schedule for her care.'

Tally experienced her first pang of compassion for Oleia's daughter. She'd had a friend at school who'd suffered from eczema and knew how distressing it could be to live with a skin condition that could cause intense irritation. 'That's good. Maybe given some time the treatment will help,' she said brittlely, striving to behave as though they were sharing a perfectly normal conversation. 'How's the nanny coping?'

'She's only providing temporary cover and will be replaced by another nanny tomorrow.' As Tally frowned Sander compressed his handsome mouth in agreement. 'It's far from ideal, but that's the best arrangement I was able to make at short notice.'

'We sound like polite strangers,' Tally commented unevenly, dismayed by the fact that they were both walking on eggshells.

And without the smallest warning of his intent, Sander reached for her. Stunning golden eyes smouldering like flames below the fringe of his lush black lashes, he banded his arms round her to lock her into contact with his lean muscular length and, lowering his arrogant dark head, he kissed her with a studied eroticism she would not have been able to resist two days earlier. But there was a cold, unresponsive stone inside her where her heart had once raced and Tally froze and flinched, refusing to feel anything.

Just as suddenly she pushed him away and stepped back to emphasise her point. 'No,' she told him flatly.

'You're here, you're with me,' Sander pointed out huskily. 'Why not?'

Shock and annoyance at being challenged like that ricocheted through Tally. 'You know why not.'

'What's the point of trying to punish me for something that happened well over a year ago while we were living apart?' Sander demanded.

Hectic colour was forced into Tally's cheeks. She could barely credit his nerve, but she also recognised that Sander's hot-blooded libido required little in the way of encouragement. 'I am not trying to punish you, Sander.'

'You're pushing me away again and I won't accept it,' he gritted with a flash of even white teeth against his bronzed skin while he surveyed her with hard masculine tenacity as though she were a puzzle that sufficient contemplation might resolve.

'You may not have a choice.'

'There is always a choice and this is not one that you are going to make for me,' Sander intoned, his Greek accent very strong as he made that admonition. 'You're still my wife—'

Tally folded her arms defensively. 'On paper—'

'Yesterday, we were on a mattress, *not* on paper,' Sander reminded her with sardonic cool. 'You chose to come back to me. You were willing then to give our marriage another chance.'

That unwelcome reminder made her small face set hard as ice in a polar blast, her pride squirming with mortification. 'It's not quite that simple.'

Sander towered over her, all the stubborn aggression

of his strong temperament in his challenging stance. 'It's exactly that simple.'

Angry resentment at the level of his scorching confidence roared through Tally in a dizzy rush and without even pausing to think about it she hit back as hard as she could. 'Well, actually, it's anything but simple. If it wasn't for the pressure that Anatole put on me, I would never have come back to you in the first place!'

Ebony brows pleating in mystification at that declaration, Sander frowned down at her. 'What are you talking about? What's your father got to do with anything?'

And, just as quickly, a sharp pang of regret infiltrated Tally, for she had never intended to tell him that truth.

'Tally…' Sander prompted impatiently.

She breathed in deep, recognising that she had boxed herself into a corner with her taunt. Now she had no alternative other than to tell him the whole story. 'Mum did something dishonest when she was living in Monaco. She had debts and to pay them she forged cheques that belonged to Roger, the man she was living with. When he found out, he threw her out and sent a solicitor to tell her that if she didn't repay the money she had stolen the police would be involved,' she explained ruefully. 'Of course, Crystal didn't have any money and I wasn't in a position to help either. Everything I've got is tied up in the business.'

Sander was frowning but her admission about Crystal's dishonesty did not appear to have surprised him that much. 'Why didn't you come to me for help? She's your mother and I would've understood.'

'Because, at the end of the day, I'm not sure there's

much to choose between you and my father. Neither of you is a fan of the something-for-nothing concept. You're both tough businessmen. My father thinks being married is good for me. He agreed to give me the money to replace what Crystal stole if I agreed to give our marriage another go. Just as Anatole wanted something in return for his generosity, I assumed that you would as well.'

As she spoke Sander's vibrant skin tone had slowly taken on an ashen shade as his natural healthy colour receded. 'I wouldn't have chosen to hold your mother's fraud over your head and blackmail you into coming back to me.'

Tally looked unimpressed. 'You like to get what you want when you want it. I'm not so sure…'

'You may be sure in this instance.' His bright eyes flared to a hot gold that positively sizzled between the curling luxuriance of his black lashes. 'I wouldn't bloody well want *any* woman on terms which meant I had to bribe her to be with me!' he shot back at her in fierce rebuttal. 'That includes you.'

'Oh…is that a fact?' Tally fielded, although she was more shaken by the strength of his reaction than she was prepared to show.

'I would've given you that money without strings attached,' Sander informed her, still very much taken aback by what he had just learned. 'Crystal is not self-supporting and never has been. I knew that when I married you and I knew she would need my help sooner or later. I'll take care of repaying Anatole.' His dark brows drew together in a heavy frown. 'Is that the only reason you came back to me? Because your father demanded it as condition of your receiving that money?'

Almost energised by the fact that she was the one surprising him for a change, Tally sent him an unapologetic look of challenge. 'Anatole seems to be convinced that if I divorce you I'll end up on my own like Mum and never settle down again. Obviously he likes to see you as a stabilising influence.'

Long black lashes dipping low over his shrewd gaze, Sander swung away, his lean hands clenching into fists as he swallowed back a guttural surge of outraged Greek condemnation. His wily father-in-law was responsible for negotiating his wife's return to his side. That was who he had to thank for his second chance at marriage. Dark fury made Sander light-headed. He wanted to hammer the wall until it cracked beneath the force of his anger and wounded pride. The blood was pulsing hotly through his veins and the pounding behind his brow made him feel as though a steel band were tightening round his temples. It took tremendous self-discipline for him to suppress his rage.

'And what was the price that bought you back into my bed?' Sander murmured with lethal cool, turning back to her with eyes dark as pitch and with no glimmer of volatile gold showing.

'That's not how it was,' Tally protested stiffly, beginning to wish that she had kept her mouth shut and resenting that sarcastic comment calculated to make her feel like a slut.

'How much?' Sander pressed with harsh emphasis.

And she told him in the hope of closing the subject.

It was a paltry amount on Sander's terms. He whistled long and low under his breath and rested derisive golden eyes on her strained face. 'No offence intended, but I got you back on the cheap. I'm surprised that you didn't turn to Robert Miller for help. I think he would have enjoyed the opportunity to ride to your rescue like a knight on a white charger.'

'I didn't want to drag Robert into my family problems. Mum was guilty of fraud, she *stole*… approaching Robert didn't seem appropriate,' Tally told him uneasily.

'So once again we owe the ongoing fact of our marriage to your father's scheming.' Sander released an unappreciative laugh. 'Anatole's good at intrigue and so are you, *moli mou*. It didn't even occur to me to suspect that you might have another motivation when you agreed to come back to me.' His darkly shadowed, strong jaw line hardened, his sensual mouth twisting. 'It's most unlike me to be naïve, but clearly I *was* naïve not to appreciate that you have your price like every other woman I've ever met.'

Her colour receded, her fine bone structure prominent as she fought to retain her composure. If it was his intent to make her feel cheap and easy he had succeeded with that cynical crack about her moral fibre. In her heart, Tally had long since accepted that her father's proposition had merely given her the excuse to do what she wanted to do anyway. She had wanted Sander back but, being too proud to admit the fact, had found it easier to tell herself that she was only returning to him because her father had given her no other choice. What did that say about her? The extent of her self-deception shamed her but in the current climate wild horses could not have dragged that truth out of her and made her share it with him. Her head high, her eyes cloaked in self-defence, she spun on her heel and headed back to her room.

Left with his own company again, Sander fought the depth of his outrage and poured a stiff drink. He tried to concentrate on practicalities. Naturally he would have to repay Anatole the sum of money the older man had expended to save Crystal's skin. These days Crystal was more her son-in-law's responsibility than Anatole's. Sander had often suspected that Tally must have suffered a cruelly insecure childhood, for her mother was selfish and irresponsible. Yet Tally had never held Crystal's flaws against her.

In fact, when it came to the people she loved, Tally had a generous and forgiving spirit. Sander had once taken it for granted that his wife loved him but that conviction had died in the aftermath of their child's death. Now he was dismally conscious that he no longer qualified for a place within her select trusted circle, but he was even more aware that he did not want a wife who had not chosen to be with him of her own free will.

By the second drink he was wondering if he was being entirely honest with himself on that score. After all, men had fought for and held onto women who weren't mad about them for centuries. Although, it must have been less of a challenge when a wife had had fewer human rights, he reasoned ruefully.

Not even history, however, demanded that he stand back and allow his wife to entertain her lover at his home. Robert Miller was taking advantage of the situation, coming to call and doubtless planning to strike at the optimum moment. Miller was a tactician. Of course he would strike when Sander's marriage was struggling to survive. It was hard to think of that sad little scrap of humanity upstairs being the cause of so much trouble.

*His* daughter, Sander reflected bleakly, was threatening to cost him his marriage but that did not release him from his responsibility towards her. In any case, a more cynical voice reminded him, the reconciliation that he had had such touching faith in had proved to be nothing but hot air. And who was to say how long the reconciliation would have lasted in such circumstances? Sander squared his broad shoulders, acknowledging the unwelcome truth that Tally had been manipulated by her father into putting her mother's needs ahead of her own. It was a truth that stung his fierce pride like acid. Most probably, Tally had shared his bed in Morocco because sex was part and parcel of any reconciliation…

# CHAPTER NINE

TALLY awoke after another bad dream with a choking sob trapped in her throat.

In the darkness of a strange room it took her a whole minute to find the bedside light. After turning it on, she withdrew her trembling hand from the switch and breathed in slow and deep in an effort to calm her racing heartbeat. Refusing to toss and turn while she struggled to forget the disturbing images in her nightmare, she decided to get up and make herself a cup of tea. There was no way that she was going to let those bad dreams take over her life again. Sliding out of bed, she put on her wrap and left the room.

Lights illuminated the floor above and for a moment Tally stood still to listen. Sadly, Lili was still crying, although the sound was much more muted than it had been earlier. Beyond it she could hear the deeper tone of an adult voice speaking. In a sudden movement, Tally turned and headed for the stairs to the upper floor. The way she had been behaving, anyone might be forgiven for thinking that she was scared of Oleia's daughter! She was just being nosy, she told herself irritably, and she was also feeling extremely sorry for the youthful nanny who was being left to cope with a baby who would not settle. It was also possible that if she actually *saw* the baby and put a face to her, she would stop having the nightmare, she reasoned tautly.

But as Tally reached the landing she realised in surprise that the voice she could hear was a man's rather than a woman's. She padded quietly along the corridor and came to a halt when she saw that it was Sander standing with his back to the half-open door and the baby draped like a small sagging sack over one broad shoulder. Ironically it was Sander she found herself staring at then, rather than the child. Her tall, well-built husband was barefoot, clad in well-worn denims and a loose linen shirt, and he was pacing the floor in an apparent attempt to soothe the child.

'Life *will* get better,' Sander was saying bracingly, one large hand patting Lili's back in a strikingly clumsy gesture while she vented a drowsy moaning complaint against his shoulder. 'I'm good at most things,' he assured the baby without false humility. 'I may not look like I've got much to offer but I'm a fast learner. If I work at being a father, I will succeed.'

Pleasantly surprised by that determined aspiration on Sander's part, Tally studied the little red swollen face below the hedgehog fuzz of curly black hair. She could see no resemblance to either Oleia or Sander in those features. Another mournful cry escaped Lili, her tiny mouth opening and closing again, her unhappiness unconcealed.

'I know what's important. If you're in trouble I'll always be there for you and even if you're in the wrong

I'll *still* be there for you,' Sander intoned intently, clearly having thought in depth about his future role. 'I won't expect you to be perfect. I won't compare you to anyone else. You can be who you want to be with me.'

Touched by what she was hearing, Tally fell back out of view, reluctant to let him see her listening because she knew it would deeply embarrass him. Everything Sander was so keen to offer Lili clearly and simply emphasised the flaws in his own relationship with his parents and he was obviously very aware of those shortcomings. He had continually been judged second-best to his older brother, Titos, who had died before Tally had come into his life. Indeed, his parents had never seemed to approve of anything Sander did and that had included his decision to marry Tally when she was pregnant. It touched Tally's heart that he was already striving to ensure that he offered his motherless daughter more support than he had ever received.

Having reached certain conclusions that made her feel uncomfortable, Tally was no longer in the mood to seek out a cup of tea and she went straight back to bed. Oleia's daughter was a harmless baby in no way responsible for her parents' behaviour, she reflected ruefully. Lili was a little person in her own right, an unhappy child who had already suffered far too many distressing changes in her short existence. Tally could not resent Lili and yet tears of regret still stung her eyes because she could not help thinking that if their son had survived Sander would have made a fine father to him, too. If he could promise to do what was right by his daughter in the midst of so much conflict, he would hardly have offered less to his first child.

Tally then asked herself the question she had been putting to the back of her mind: how would she feel if she were shortly to discover that she had already fallen pregnant again? They had used no form of contraception in Morocco. The current hitch in her menstrual cycle—she was late—might simply be the result of foreign travel and the emotional upheaval she had suffered. But, on the other hand, it could equally well be the first sign that she had conceived for the second time. On the most basic level her heart leapt at the very idea, but on another level she was distressed by the suspicion that their marriage might already be on the rocks again. If that was true she would not be able to give her child the secure background she had been so keen to supply. In the space of days, with the revelation of Lili's existence, their lives had changed radically and nothing she could do could change that.

The following morning, Sander had left for his London office by the time that Tally came downstairs. She received several sympathetic texts from her sister, Cosima, which made her think warmly about the younger girl and she arranged to see her the next week. Robert Miller, her business partner, drove up to the house on the stroke of noon in a sleek Aston Martin and suggested they talk over lunch at a local restaurant.

Climbing back into his sports car, Robert dealt her slim figure an appreciative appraisal. 'For someone who has had a tough couple of days you look amazingly well.'

'Thanks.' Her whipped cream skin delicately flushed below the straight fall of her dark marmalade hair, Tally withheld the information that Sander was responsible for her fashionable turquoise skirt and fitted top. He had great taste in clothes and was rather more adventurous with colour than she was. 'I'm very resilient.'

It was a relief when Robert concentrated on business and while they discussed the monthly returns of her design firm at length over a light meal her tension over the questions she had feared he might ask slowly evaporated. She always enjoyed Robert's company and in recent months had wondered on several occasions how she might have felt about Robert had she met him *before* she met Sander. Tall, dark-haired and with bright blue eyes, he was an attractive man and a very successful one, but he had simply not registered on her feminine radar while Sander was around.

Was she one of those women who preferred a bad boy who set her a challenge? Sander had always been a challenge in one way or another. Volatile and unpredictable, he had once seriously doubted the ties that commitment entailed. Although he had married her he had not fallen in love with her. Yet she had fallen like a ton of bricks for him and suffered accordingly. Or was it more a case of her having made a rod for her own back?

For the first time, Tally looked at the other side of the equation. Had her awareness that he would not give her those words of love encouraged the growing disenchantment and distrust on her part that in the aftermath of tragedy had ultimately led to their estrangement? She had held his initial unwillingness to embrace fatherhood against him to the bitter end, hadn't she? He had not loved her and therefore she had found it easier to believe the worst of him, assuming that he could not possibly be grieving for the child they had lost in the same way that she was. Grief had torn them apart because they had not shared it.

All of a sudden she was painfully conscious that Lili's advent could affect them in a similar manner. If they did not share the consequences of her arrival in their lives how could their relationship hope to survive? There could be few more divisive factors than the need for a wife to accept another woman's child. Yet, all over the world thousands of women did exactly that, Tally conceded in exasperation. Step-families, cobbled together from broken and new relationships, were common and many people found themselves raising children to whom they were not related. Such relationships could be particularly challenging and more prone to breakdown and she now fully understood why that was so.

After all, Tally had once expected to be the mother of Sander's first living child! In addition she had been jealous of Oleia and her history of intimacy with Sander. Oleia might be dead but Lili was the ongoing proof of that intimacy. *Get over it*, a little voice said harshly inside her head. Had not she walked out on their marriage? Leaving the door open for Oleia and Lili's conception? Now she needed to concentrate on the bigger picture and acknowledge that Lili was reliant on the goodwill of the adults surrounding her. How much goodwill was she willing to offer that little baby?

For possibly the first time, Tally recognised that she

could not have Sander without his daughter. After all, she did not expect him to neglect his child or to give her up, did she? This wasn't a competition, was it? She also knew that she would never ask him to keep his distance from Lili in the same way that her father's wife had zealously sought to exclude her from Anatole's life. Her father had married a possessive woman who felt threatened by Tally's very existence. There and then, Tally resolved to be more mature and just in her dealings with Sander's daughter.

'You're very quiet,' Robert remarked on the drive back to the manor.

'I have a lot on my mind,' Tally confessed.

'You shouldn't be beating yourself up about something that has nothing to do with you,' Robert pronounced decisively. 'You need a fresh start.'

Tally raised a wry brow. *'Another* one?'

'Walk away from him,' Robert advised as he switched off the car engine outside the house. 'Right now, your marriage is in a disaster zone and nobody could expect you to make a go of it.'

Uncomfortable with the conversation, Tally climbed out. Robert followed suit and strode round the front of his car to reach out and grip her hands in his.

'I can't discuss this kind of stuff with you,' Tally protested.

'You deserve better. You were only weeks away from getting a divorce when you went back to him,' Robert reminded her urgently.

The sound of the front door opening made Tally's head swivel, green eyes widening in dismay when she saw Sander striding towards them. She tried to tug her fingers free of the other man's hold but he had too tight a hold on her hands.

'You've got nothing to apologise for and no reason to hide our relationship,' Robert told her insistently.

'Get your hands off my wife!' Sander growled from several feet away.

Tally clashed with scorchingly angry golden eyes and her heartbeat accelerated.

'You're in the middle of a divorce!' Robert pronounced witheringly. 'You don't own her any more.'

'Nobody owns me,' Tally pointed out drily, hoping to lend a note of common sense to the scene developing as she finally managed to pull her hands free and gave her business partner a look of reproach. 'I belong to me.'

'Walk away, Tally,' Sander instructed between clenched teeth, inflamed by the reality that Tally had not disagreed with Miller when he stated that they were still in the middle of a divorce.

'I'm not going anywhere if there's going to be some stupid male confrontation,' Tally announced, her chin tilting in warning. 'I'll see you next week, Robert—'

'Come back to London with me now,' Robert suggested. 'You can't *want* to stay here…'

Sander closed a lean brown hand like a manacle over Tally's wrist. 'She's not leaving. She stays with me.'

Watching the two men square up to each other, Tally just wanted to scream in exasperation. She could feel the pent-up aggression in Sander in the taut clench of his long fingers and the poised readiness of his stance. He was a very physical man and in his current angry mood as unstable as gelignite. 'It would be better if you just went home, Robert.' She sighed.

'Why? Are you not allowed visitors now either?' Robert demanded, evidently happy to fan the flames.

In an abrupt movement, Tally tore her hand free of Sander's and spun to stalk into the house, her rigid back expressing her frustration with all things male. If she was the source of the bad feeling, her removal from the scenario ought to calm matters down, she reasoned, turning in the hall to gaze out through a side window. She was just in time to see Robert punch Sander and shock froze her to the spot because she had assumed Sander was the more likely of the two to lose his temper. Sander, however, wasted no time in striking back and as Robert went down on one knee on the gravel Tally raced back outside again to intervene.

'*Stop it!*' she screamed furiously. 'There's nothing worth fighting over—'

Frowning, Sander rested stunning dark golden eyes on her. 'You're worth fighting for,' he contradicted almost conversationally.

'If you hit him again, I'm leaving you!' Tally threatened him in desperation.

In the interim, Robert had lunged at Sander again and, taken by surprise, Sander went down heavily. That was when Tally recognised just how much she was still in love with her husband because she almost waded into the midst of the fight and was on the very brink of thumping Robert for taking unfair advantage.

'Just go, Robert!' Tally yelled shakily.

Wiping blood off his lip, her business partner shot

her a rueful appraisal, her protective stance not having escaped his attention. 'I'm wasting my time here.'

'Yes, leave before I kill you,' Sander advised rawly as he sprang upright again.

Breathing in shallow spurts, Tally watched while Robert drove off and then she turned to frown at Sander. 'He did hit you first, didn't he?' she checked.

Sander gave her a considering look and then grimaced slowly as if he was picking his words with extreme care. 'Not exactly—'

'You mean, *you* started the fight?' Tally flared, furious that she had not grasped this salient fact sooner.

'You're my wife and he had stepped over the line,' Sander reasoned without remorse.

'If you'd stayed out of things, nothing would have happened!' Tally launched back at him. 'He was just trying to talk to me.'

Sander's dark golden eyes hardened. 'He was making a move on you.'

Stepping back indoors at a smart pace powered by annoyance, Tally slung him a look of condemnation. 'Whether he was or not is none of your business!'

'Tally…'

She spun back to him in the airy entrance hall.

Sander rested his brooding gaze to her. 'I realise that this is a difficult situation for you but we are still married.'

Green eyes veiling, she nodded slowly, her temper too uncertain for her to trust herself to speak. She was not prepared to argue about Robert. It was one thing to allow Sander to wonder exactly what her relationship with the other man entailed but quite another to wilfully add to a heated misunderstanding.

Sander released his pent-up breath in a measured hiss. 'Maybe what you need most right now is a break from me.'

Green eyes glinting, her head came up. 'That's very possible.'

'I need to have a face-to-face meeting with a man I'm hoping to do business with in Athens. But that would mean leaving you here in charge of Lili and her new nanny for at least forty-eight hours,' Sander advanced grimly.

'I can handle that,' Tally heard herself claim, sooner than admit that she had not yet worked up sufficient courage to enter the same room as Oleia's child.

His ebony brows drew together, his surprise patent at that response. 'You *can*?'

'Why not? I'm not so perverse as to hold Lili's parentage against her!' Tally claimed with pride.

'If that's true, you're behaving with extraordinary restraint, *moli mou*.'

Her cheeks reddened as she was conscious that she had only become more rational about the issue that very same day.

'I mean it.' Sander regarded her with level dark golden eyes. 'I couldn't handle you having a child with Robert Miller. I couldn't handle that at all.'

And his generosity in admitting that fact made her equally generous as she appreciated the concerns that her defiant silence on that subject had caused him. 'As

I haven't slept with Robert, the situation could never arise.'

A sudden startling smile flashed across Sander's beautifully shaped mouth, chasing the raw tension from his lean, hard-boned features. His stunning eyes were bright below the fringe of his luxuriant lashes. 'Thank you for telling me that. You didn't have to.'

And Tally was guiltily aware at that instant that Sander would never have had a fight with Robert had he known that her relationship with her business partner was still of the platonic variety. Sexual jealousy had fired his aggression. When Sander took his leave an hour later she was working on a pitch for a client. Almost as soon as the helicopter had taken off, she closed her laptop and stood up. It was past time that she met Sander's daughter.

The latest nanny, a capable-looking brunette in her late twenties, was changing Lili in the nursery. Her palms damp with nerves, Tally entered the room and introduced herself as Sander's wife. The angry patches of irritation she could see marring the baby's exposed skin soon banished her self-consciousness.

'No wonder she cries!' Tally exclaimed, dismayed by the extent of Lili's eczema. 'Poor little girl…'

'Regular massage with oil may help,' the nanny remarked helpfully. 'Pure cotton clothing and bedding can help as well.'

'I'll get hold of some,' Tally promised immediately, delighted to have a practical aspect to focus on.

'Would you mind looking after her while I go

downstairs and get my lunch?' the brunette asked apologetically.

'Of course not.' In truth Tally was more embarrassed that although it was late afternoon nobody had thought to relieve the nanny for a meal break. But then, who was there to think of such things? Sander was struggling with the responsibility and ignorant of what it took to fully look after the needs of so young a child. If Lili was to be tended round the clock by staff alone, a second nanny would have to be employed.

Lili was planted into Tally's arms without fanfare. She was a tiny child, not weighing much at all. As, true to form, the little girl began to cry again Tally drew in a deep steadying breath and reminded herself that she had always liked children and babies in particular. Once the nanny had departed, her reticence evaporated and she rocked the baby and talked to her quietly. Sad little dark eyes looked up at her curiously. Tally took a seat and extended a rattle to Lili to engage her interest. A tiny hand grasped the item. Time ticked on while Tally sat there feeling amazingly calm and enjoying the baby's warmth in her arms in a way she had not realised she would. Lili's lashes gradually drooped, her hold on the rattle loosening, and eventually she drifted off to sleep.

The nanny reappeared and cheerfully removed the slumbering baby to the cot. In a bit of a daze, Tally stood there gazing down at Lili. Her heartstrings had been tugged by the tiny girl's helplessness and unquestioning trust in her. There and then, she promised herself that whatever happened in her marriage she would not blame Oleia's daughter for it. She loved Sander. How could she refuse to accept his child?

That night Tally slept right through without any bad dreams. The next day she travelled up to London in a limousine. She visited her office, met a client at her town house and presented her with a scheme, before she went shopping on Lili's behalf—purchasing pure cotton sleep suits and cot linen that would not chafe the baby's tender skin. Before she headed back to Roxburn Manor, she called in at her apartment and packed a case. The necessities taken care of, she returned to the manor and only then did it occur to her that she should have made an appointment to see her doctor while she was in London. It was time, she recognised, to have a pregnancy test. She rang up and made an appointment.

Although Sander had received several messages from his parents alerting him to the fact that they wanted to speak to him, he had not responded, nor had he visited them while he was in Greece. He knew why they wanted to speak to him but he wasn't a rebellious teenager in need of a lecture about fathering Lili. As far as he was concerned the only person he needed to explain himself to on that score was Tally and he was not entirely sure that Tally would still be at Roxburn Manor when he returned.

'My wife?' he asked Mrs Jones, the housekeeper, barely one step through the front door.

'In the nursery, sir,' the older woman told him.

Sander mounted the stairs two at a time. That Tally might actually be with Lili was more than he had hoped for. Before he reached the second floor he heard Tally's soft voice speaking and when he walked into the nursery he was taken aback to see his baby daughter lying on a towel on Tally's lap being massaged with oil.

'She's not crying,' he breathed in wonderment.

'She likes this,' Tally told him, dipping her fingers in the tub of emulsified oil and working carefully over a skinny little leg until it glistened.

Sander gazed down at Lili's face, which was turned on its side and more peaceful than he had ever seen it.

'She usually goes to sleep afterwards. After a massage session she's much calmer,' Tally advanced, glancing up at her handsome husband and staring, for while she had appreciated the privacy in which to get acquainted with Lili, life without Sander in it was like champagne without the fizz, irretrievably and boringly flat.

'So are you, *moli mou*,' Sander could not resist telling her.

'Lili doesn't deserve my anger,' Tally whispered, compressing her generous mouth as she gently fed the baby's limbs into a sleepsuit. 'I've made an appointment for her with a new dermatologist. I've been reading a book on eczema and I thought it might be worth getting some allergy tests done in case something she's eating or is in contact with is aggravating the condition.'

His dark, deep set eyes semi-screened by his lashes, he breathed, 'You have no idea how much I appreciate you taking an interest in her.'

'It makes me feel better, so it's selfish as well,' Tally muttered, uneasy in receipt of his praise, because she wasn't proud of the struggle she'd had before her better nature had overcome more selfish promptings.

They dined less formally than usual in a room only across the corridor from the kitchen. The meal was simple but beautifully cooked and presented. Tally had had a chat with the housekeeper and had admitted that she and Sander were not great fans of pomp and ceremony. Mrs Jones had confided that she would need more staff to meet the high standards laid down by Sander's mother and together the two women had agreed a more casual approach for what remained of Sander and Tally's stay.

'Did you visit your parents?' Tally enquired over the meal.

'I ought to have done, but I didn't.' Sander grimaced. 'I wasn't in the mood to be put through a four-act tragedy about Lili.'

He had changed into jeans and a shirt but black stubble still outlined his stubborn jaw line, accentuating the wilful sensuality of his shapely mouth. On several occasions when Tally's mind outran her self-discipline, her attention would linger on his lean, darkly handsome face and that little knot of excitement that Sander could always evoke would tighten low in her pelvis—reminding her of needs and urges she had suppressed since Lili had arrived in their lives. Desire burned through her like a hot knife piercing butter.

It was the nanny's night off and later that evening Tally was giving Lili a bottle when Sander appeared in the doorway. 'I should be doing that,' he stated without noticeable enthusiasm.

'Well, you should know *how*,' Tally agreed calmly,

choosing to take the comment at face value and standing up to indicate that he should take her place.

Put on the spot, Sander breathed in deep as Tally settled his daughter into his arms and showed him how to hold the child and angle the feeding bottle. 'She's so tiny,' he complained, clearly fearful of hurting the baby in some way.

'It's not rocket science,' she told him.

She collided involuntarily with his stunning dark golden eyes and felt a kernel of heat sizzle through her nerve endings. Ready colour warmed her cheeks and she glanced away again, embarrassed by her susceptibility.

'She looks quite cute when she's not crying,' Sander murmured in surprise.

'She's feeding better. When she puts on some weight she'll look more like a baby should. She's always very anxious, as well. I think she's had too many different people caring for her,' Tally commented, smoothing gentle fingertips over Lili's little furrowed brow to soothe her. The baby's flickering dark eyes swivelled to Tally and remained glued to her for the remainder of the feeding session.

Tally settled Lili back in her cot and went to bed, wondering if Sander would join her there. She lay there watching the door, thinking about him, *wanting* him, *willing* him. She stayed awake a long time before she accepted that Sander had no plans to share the bed with her. Soon after that the baby listener warned her that Lili was awake and needed settling again. It was the middle of the night before Tally, tired and cross as she was, finally slept.

A sunny day was shining behind the curtains when Sander shook her awake again. Pushing tousled hair out of her eyes, Tally sat up and frowned at him. 'What time is it?'

'Ten. My parents are here—'

A rocket attack could not have got Tally out of bed more efficiently. The very prospect of facing his exquisitely groomed mother without proper notice filled her with panic. 'Oh, my goodness! What do they want?'

Sander's handsome mouth tightened into a hard line of derision. 'Apparently, they want Lili…'

# CHAPTER TEN

THAT staggering announcement sent Tally careening into the bathroom to wash and dash on some make-up. What had he meant by that outrageous statement? Were the older couple actually offering to step in and bring Oleia's daughter up for Sander? Tally was astonished by the suggestion, for his parents had not impressed her as being particularly fond of children. When she emerged from the bathroom within ten minutes to an empty bedroom, she wasted no time in pulling on jeans and a black tee, reluctant to waste any more time in making herself presentable. Sander had already returned downstairs to entertain his parents.

When Tally joined the three of them in the drawing room, Mrs Jones was serving coffee and biscuits and Eirene Volakis was saying to her son with her usual indifference to the presence of staff, 'If only you had married Oleia when you had the chance. She would have been so perfect for you.'

Her flawless skin staining with colour, Tally came to a sudden awkward halt. Her mother-in-law gave her an acidic smile that acknowledged her presence and no more.

'I don't think so. We split up when we were young because we were completely incompatible,' Sander imparted smoothly.

'We were always very fond of Oleia,' Petros Volakis declared cheerfully. 'That's one reason why we're willing to offer her child a home with us.'

'In the circumstances your wife can hardly want her,' Eirene contended without embarrassment.

'Lili is Sander's daughter,' Tally declared firmly.

Sander's mother elevated an unimpressed brow. 'The child would be much better off with us. I've always wanted a little girl. When I was carrying Sander, I was convinced I was going to have a daughter,' she admitted, shooting her son an accusing look as if his gender were somehow his fault. 'I was devastated when I had another son instead.'

'That was a source of great disappointment,' Petros agreed, giving his wife a sympathetic look.

Tally could not bite her tongue any longer. 'And neither of you ever got over it, did you? Is that why you always favoured your elder son over the younger? Is that why you never have a good word to say about Sander?' she condemned.

Sander was startled and embarrassed by Tally's spirited intercession on his behalf. Faint colour edged his superb cheekbones. 'Let's not have this conversation.'

'You have no manners,' Eirene Volakis informed Tally icily.

'My wife has excellent manners,' Sander countered crisply. 'From my own point of view, I'm very surprised that you should want to take on the burden of a child at your stage in life and I don't think it's a good idea.'

'We could equip Lili with everything she requires to take her place in the highest stratum of Greek society,' Sander's mother pronounced haughtily.

'There are more important things,' Sander replied drily.

'Not to me,' his elegant mother told him. 'She would thrive in our care and why not? She *is* our first grandchild.'

'Actually my son was,' Tally could not refrain from slotting in.

Sander's father had the decency to give Tally an apologetic look but Eirene treated her to a stony appraisal, unmoved by that reminder.

Tally focused on Sander, recognising the tension hardening his lean strong face, and she wondered if his parents' proposition secretly appealed to him. A knock sounded on the door and Sander strode across the room to open it. The nanny came in with Lili cradled in her comfortable baby carrier.

'It really is time that I became acquainted with my granddaughter,' Eirene Volakis announced in a saccharin-sweet voice as she approached the child.

The older woman then came to a sudden halt and exclaimed, 'What on earth is the matter with her face?'

'Lili suffers from eczema,' Tally explained.

'It's very unsightly,' Eirene said critically, her mouth curling into a little moue of distaste as she studied the patches of inflamed skin that marred the baby's cheek and chin. 'Will it clear up?'

'Some babies grow out of it, others don't, I'm afraid. We can only wait and see,' Tally answered and she fought a protective urge to whip Lili out of the carrier and cuddle her in the face of her grandmother's disparagement.

Sardonic amusement flashed through Sander's expressive eyes as his parent drew back from his daughter as though the child's condition might prove to be contagious. 'I'm sorry she's not perfect,' he said with quiet derision.

Stiffening at that scornful note, the older woman frowned. 'She's not a healthy child. Perhaps it would be best if she remained with you.'

'It scarcely matters as I'm not prepared to hand her over to anyone,' Sander asserted quietly. 'Oleia entrusted me with her daughter and I intend to bring her up. How Lili looks makes no difference to me or Tally.'

Eirene Volakis appeared unimpressed but her husband could not hide his embarrassment at the speed with which his wife had withdrawn her plan to give Lili a home. Clearly, only the prettiest little girls might apply for such a position. Tally soothed the baby when she started crying, Lili had been wakened from a nap to be brought downstairs and introduced to her grandparents. Within fifteen minutes, their visitors had departed again, all interest in the child abandoned.

Sander crouched down to restore Lili's rattle to her hand when it dropped and she cried for it, little starfish fingers stretching unavailingly for her lost toy. 'You're stuck with us, Lili. It appears we can't even give you away.'

'Don't say that, even jokingly,' Tally scolded.

'She's not unsightly,' Sander declared, tight-mouthed with annoyance at that remark.

'No, she's not.'

'Were you hoping I'd hand her over to them?' Sander shot the question at her without warning.

Tally tensed at that blunt demand and the keen appraisal that accompanied it and had to admit that only a few days earlier she might have given him a different answer. 'Absolutely not. I don't think your mother is capable of offering a child unconditional love.'

'She never admitted that before—that she had hoped I would be a daughter,' Sander reflected with a sudden frowning shake of his handsome dark head. 'I was the most energetic and noisy little boy. No wonder I was always irritating her.'

And very probably one of the very few disappointments a rich and spoiled woman like Eirene Volakis had ever had to endure, Tally mused, pained by the knowledge that Sander had been so unappreciated as a child. 'No wonder you're independent.'

'Let's go back to London tomorrow,' Sander suggested, dropping the subject of his family at understandable speed. 'Since yesterday, the paps have been chasing a politician caught playing away from his wife. Lili is old news now.'

'It would certainly be easier to get back to work,' Tally conceded.

As she registered that they were talking like polite strangers again Tally's eyes stung like mad, forcing her to blink furiously. In Morocco she had gone to Sander, making the first move to bridge the distance between them, but she was not prepared to go the same route again. He didn't love her. The least she had to do to hold her own in such an unequal relationship was hang onto her dignity. She shrank from the prospect of mentioning her need for a pregnancy test. Those bright happy days at the villa in Morocco when having another child had seemed such a wonderful idea were long gone. Having once before broken such news to Sander when it was unwelcome, she could not face finding herself in a similar position again.

That evening, her father phoned and asked her to meet him for lunch again, but at his hotel rather than at the usual restaurant. Surprised, because it was unusual for her to see or hear from Anatole Karydas so soon after their last meeting, Tally wondered if he was planning to ask her about Lili and hoped that she was wrong. She wasn't ready to talk about the situation. Although she had come to terms as best she could with Lili's existence, she and Sander were still estranged. Yet she had no idea how that had happened in the wake of their happiness in Morocco.

As soon as Lili and her nanny had settled into the town house the next day and Sander had left for the office, Tally went to her father's hotel. Anatole treated her to sandwiches and tea in his hotel suite and from the minute she walked through the door his discomfiture was plain. He began to speak several times and then fell silent again.

'What is it?' Tally finally pressed.

'I'm not very good at apologising,' the older man

admitted frankly. 'But I got it wrong with you and Sander. I shouldn't have interfered. I shouldn't have used Crystal's financial difficulties as a means of coercion.'

'No, you shouldn't have done,' Tally agreed with much of his own directness.

'Obviously, after what's happened…this child that's turned up,' her father specified with a dismissive motion of his hand that made it clear that he had no desire to get any deeper into that touchy subject, 'I wouldn't dream of trying to hold you to the terms I insisted on. The money is gone, forget about it. Sander is determined to repay it and won't take no for an answer. I must say he's the only one of the Volakis tribe who has any real backbone.'

Involuntarily, Tally smiled at that compliment. 'Yes, he's got a lot of that.'

Anatole frowned. 'But you should never have told him that I was responsible for your decision to return to your marriage. I expect you didn't think it mattered after that shocking revelation about Oleia Telis and her baby was made public, but no man would deal well with such humiliating news.'

Her brow indented in surprise. 'Sander's never mentioned it again since I told him so I don't think it had that big an impact on him…'

'For a young man, accustomed to female adulation, the discovery that he owed his wife's presence to her father's interference would have been a shattering blow. It never occurred to me that you would tell him what I'd done,' the older man admitted wryly. 'That would have torpedoed any reconciliation, Tally.'

And the confidence with which he made that assurance certainly gave Tally pause for thought. At the time when she had admitted that truth, Sander had been very worked up about it, she recalled. It was possible that his silence since that day did not mean that he had simply shrugged off her admission and learned to live with it. In fact, perhaps it was her confession that she had been bribed into coming back to him that was the current biggest stumbling block in their marriage. Could that be why he was so very polite and distant?

'I have only one awkward question to ask you,' Tally confided. 'Were you aware that Sander had got involved with Oleia again?'

Anatole pursed his lips. 'No, I knew nothing of it. She left Greece to live in London, then Paris, and fell off the radar. I heard whispers about Oleia's party lifestyle and the child only after she died.'

Before they parted, her father invited her and Sander to his fiftieth birthday party in Athens. When she studied him in surprise, he admitted that he regretted being an absent parent throughout her childhood and that he wanted to put that past behind him. Tally was warmed by that declaration and her first official invitation to his marital home and went off to keep her medical appointment in a thoughtful mood.

The pregnancy test was done very quickly and within minutes Tally was in receipt of the news she had both feared and craved. She had conceived again. She was full of joy when she knew the result but also terrified that something might go wrong again. Her GP was quick to assure her that, with her past history, she would receive an early scan. Tally, however, was already planning to make an appointment with the obstetrician she had consulted before so that she could be confident that every possible resource would be utilised to try and ensure that she gave birth to a healthy child.

On the way back to the town house, Tally took a detour to visit her mother and share her news. Crystal, who had phoned her daughter for the details in the early stages of the shower of publicity that had accompanied Lili's arrival in London, was delighted. Her mother also informed her that she was in the running for a job as a buyer for a group of fashion boutiques owned by a friend and that she was moving into a place of her own.

'The clothes are aimed at my age group and I know that market very well. I'm also pretty good at negotiating prices,' Crystal pointed out with satisfaction. 'Cross your fingers for me.'

Tally was relieved that the older woman had found somewhere else to live and she'd actually been looking for employment and thought that even if her mother didn't get the job she had, at least, made a start on turning her life in a new direction.

'And with a new baby on the way, you and Sander are back on track,' her mother pronounced with satisfaction. 'Well, that's not a surprise.'

Tally raised a brow. 'Isn't it?'

'I'm not stupid, Tally,' her blonde mother pronounced with pride. 'You're mad about kids so you were sure to come round to Lili sooner rather than later. And Sander's absolutely mad about you, so of course things were sure to work out.'

'Sander's mad about me?'

'Five minutes of being single again and he can think of nothing better to do than get his wife back? That speaks for itself. I've never seen a couple happier than the two of you were earlier on in France.'

As she took leave of Crystal Tally nourished that thought and the joyful memories she still had of that period in her life. They *had* been incredibly happy together until tragedy had struck and grief brought an end to mutual understanding and tolerance, she reflected ruefully. She splayed her hand across her still-flat stomach and prayed that she would not be put through a repeat experience, that roller coaster of anticipation followed by heartbreaking loss during her first pregnancy had broken her in two. In the foyer of the block of apartments where her mother lived, she used her phone to call Sander. Unfortunately, he was in a meeting and she had to leave a message telling him that she needed to see him urgently. This time around there would be nothing apologetic about the manner in which she announced her pregnancy!

Sander entered the drawing room of their London home with all the animation of a man about to be confronted with a hangman's noose. His lean, bronzed profile pale and taut, he levelled brilliant dark eyes on Tally. 'My PA should've put your call straight through to me. What's happened?'

A slim figure clad in grey separates, her hair framing her flushed cheekbones, Tally stood up and focused bright green eyes on her husband. 'I'm pregnant…'

Sander could not hide his surprise because he had

feared that another intention lay behind her sudden desire to speak to him, and it was one of those rare occasions when he was very relieved to appreciate that he had jumped to entirely the wrong conclusion. He crossed the room in a sudden movement that took her by surprise and wrapped both arms round her to lift her up against his lean powerful body and hug her tightly to him.

'Wow...' he breathed gruffly, his beautiful dark eyes alight with unconcealed satisfaction. 'That has to be the best news I've ever heard!'

Tally was startled by his enthusiasm. 'I wasn't sure how you would feel...'

Astonished by the claim, Sander lifted his proud dark head and lowered her slowly back onto her own feet, his eyes mystified. 'Didn't we plan this baby together? Isn't this what we both wanted?'

'Well, yes, but—'

'Are you worried about how much support I'll be?' Sander interrupted worriedly, gently pressing her down on the sofa and hunkering down to study her anxious face. 'I'll be there every step of the way this time. I'm not the same guy I was a couple of years ago. I've grown up, learned what I want out of life and what's important.'

Her heart seemed to swell inside her and her throat tightened, tears prickling the backs of her eyes. 'Is that true? Is that really, truthfully how you feel now?'

Sander gripped her hand. 'Tally, when I got that message from you earlier, I was scared witless that you wanted me to come home so that you could tell me that you were leaving me again!'

Her lashes fluttered in bemusement and then she

looked at him in shock. 'But why would you think that?'

'Why wouldn't I think that?' he countered, his voice roughened by an amount of emotion he couldn't hide. 'You didn't *choose* to come back to live with me. Your father pressured you into doing it.'

'Oh, my goodness, you *were* still concerned about that,' Tally registered uncomfortably.

In answer to that comment, Sander emitted a rueful laugh of disbelief. 'How could I not be concerned about that?'

'You didn't show that you were still worried about it,' Tally reasoned semi-accusingly.

'I don't wear my heart on my sleeve, *yineka mou*. What was I going to do about it anyway? I didn't like what you told me, but if I wanted to hang onto you I had to live with it,' he pointed out ruefully. 'And, make no mistake, I wanted you to stay. I also realised that even if you were only staying married to me to please your father I was still happier to have you on those terms than to lose you altogether.'

Her eyes went very wide as she absorbed that far-reaching declaration. 'You didn't mind?'

'I minded a great deal,' Sander contradicted bluntly, his strong jaw-line clenching hard. 'I have my pride. If you didn't want to be with me I should have told you that you were free to go. But I couldn't face doing that. I couldn't face losing you again.'

Fascinated by that intense speech from a guy famous for keeping it cool, Tally lifted a forefinger to trace the hard line of his compressed lips. Her curiosity was intense. 'Couldn't you?'

'When you walked out on me in France after we lost our son I went to hell and back,' Sander admitted bleakly, his expressive eyes full of the dark shadows of the past. 'I hit the bottle hard. I felt like such a failure. You'd come through one of the worst possible experiences a woman can have and I knew I'd let you down. But I didn't know what else I could've done differently because you wouldn't let me near you and you wouldn't talk to me either.'

Tally grimaced and leant forward to wrap both arms round him in a guilty hug. 'I'm so sorry. I *did* shut you out. I think my attitude went right back to the beginning of my pregnancy when you were less than keen on the idea of becoming a father. I don't think I ever let go of my resentment of that and I should've done because you did change.'

Sander vaulted upright, carrying her with him. Strong arms closed round her, he gazed down at her with strained dark eyes. 'But not fast enough. I felt so bad about that attitude of mine after the baby died but I couldn't alter the past.'

'And I couldn't forgive you for it, which was unfair,' she whispered tearfully against his shoulder.

'It was you who taught me to want that baby,' he confided ruefully. 'I wanted him because you did. It never occurred to me that anything could go wrong and when it did, I was filled with so much guilt because I had never thought of our child as a real person. You were so desperately unhappy and I couldn't help you. That made me feel more useless than ever.'

'Is that why you started working every hour you possibly could and avoiding me?'

Sander stared down at her troubled face with pained dark eyes. 'You didn't want me any more. You made that very clear. The way I saw it, I was staying out of your way, which seemed like a good idea at the time.'

'Maybe I thought it was when I was so depressed but being lonely made everything worse,' Tally confided chokily. 'I was having those horrible dreams night after night...'

Sander grimaced. 'You wouldn't even tell me about them.'

'Those dreams were so crazy I didn't dare tell you what was in them. I was afraid I was losing my mind,' she said heavily and then she told him about how she had dreamt that she was frantically searching for their baby son who had died.

Sander was appalled. 'If only you had told me. When you moved into another bedroom I saw it as another rejection. But you were just working through the grief process. We both were, in our different ways,' Sander proffered with a grim shake of his handsome dark head. 'I just didn't know what to say to you because I felt so guilty.'

'Did Oleia make you feel better?' Tally asked him abruptly.

Sander groaned. 'Worse. I must show you the letter she left for me with her solicitor. She explained why she didn't tell me about Lili.'

Tally frowned. 'Why?' she prompted. 'And why did you turn to her in the first place? Was it just because she was gorgeous?'

His dark deep-set eyes flamed gold and he jerked a broad shoulder in a clumsy shrug. 'When you walked out on our marriage it was a massive rejection and it hurt. Oleia always made it clear that she wanted me. You didn't want me. That's how basic her attraction was,' he revealed, shame-faced.

That truth hurt Tally as well, since even in the tumultuous miasma of sorrow she had still wanted Sander but had not felt able to let that side of her nature loose while she was still grieving. She swallowed back the thickness in her throat. 'And why didn't she tell you about Lili when she realised that she was pregnant?'

'Oleia had her pride. The morning after that night,' Sander specified tautly, his brilliant eyes veiled, his deep voice clipped, 'she said to me, "You're still madly in love with your wife, aren't you?" I couldn't lie to her.'

Tally was flabbergasted by that response and its ramifications.

Sander winced. 'She was right and that's why she saw no point in telling me about Lili. It was only when she realised that her daughter had a serious skin condition that she appreciated that she had to tell me because her daughter might need her father to raise her.'

'Let me get this straight,' Tally breathed unevenly. 'You're saying you were in love with me when we were first married?'

'But I didn't realise just how important you were to me until you walked out,' Sander admitted in a driven undertone. 'After Oleia hurt me when I was a teenager I swore I would never do love again.'

'I sort of guessed that,' Tally confided.

'I thought love made a man weak and vulnerable,' Sander confessed in a raw undertone. 'I didn't intend to fall for you and I didn't know I had. Somehow you became integral to my peace of mind and happiness without me ever fully appreciating it until it was too late. I couldn't bear to live my life without you.'

'Oh, Sander...' Her throat clogged with tears, Tally rested slim fingers against his cheekbones to frame his lean strong face. 'If you love me you're never going to have to live your life without me; in fact, you're stuck with me for ever!'

'For ever has a beautiful sound to it,' Sander muttered thickly, his arms tightening round her ribcage so much that he was threatening to crush the breath from her body. 'I want you for ever. But I was so shocked when I found out about Lili. I was afraid she would finish us.'

'She could have done,' Tally conceded tightly. 'I had to search my soul to accept her at first but now I'm beginning to love her on her own account. She needs both of us.'

'You've been so generous...' His dark deep voice was thick with emotion and when she glanced up at him she registered that his dark golden eyes were shimmering with moisture. 'To her, most of all,' he continued doggedly, determined to acknowledge her kind and loving heart. 'It's made me love you even more and appreciate that I really did marry a very special woman. And now you're going to have our baby, my happiness is complete...'

A big hand splayed across her concave stomach and something of his fascination and pride shone in his eloquent gaze. His enthusiasm touched her deeply and healed the last of her doubts. She blinked back tears from her eyes and wrapped her arms round his neck, grateful that in spite of the events that had been sent to try them they had miraculously found each other again and with a love that was, after it all, much deeper and stronger than before. She had let grief take her over and exclude him and it had almost cost them their marriage, for they had not known each other well enough to surmount those obstacles. This time around they were much more aware of each other's needs.

'I love you *so* much it hurts,' she confessed.

'What *really* hurts is trying to get by without you,' Sander contradicted with the conviction of a male who had done that and, having suffered, had no intention of returning to those dark days. 'I may be a late developer in the love stakes but I do value you as you should be valued. I know what a wonderful find you are.'

'But it's very quiet in the bedroom department,' Tally remarked, tugging his tie out and working the knot loose with helpful fingers.

Sander settled shaken eyes on her. 'But you rejected me...'

'That was just one little kiss.' Tally pouted. 'A lady always reserves the right to change her mind. I never thought you would be so easily put off. What happened to all that Volakis drive and determination?'

Sander vented a startled laugh of appreciation and a wolfish grin banished his gravity. He brought his hungry mouth down on hers in a kiss that made her toes curl and her body leap joyously back to vibrant life. 'Let me *show* you, *agapi mou*...'

Eighteen months later, Tally strolled out onto the terrace with a tray of lemonade and feeding beakers for the children.

Sander was watching Lili ride her little red toy car round the courtyard as their son, Timon, toddled behind it, his little face stamped with that famous strain of Volakis determination.

'We need another toy car,' Sander forecast as both toddlers pelted across the terrace to collect beakers of juice and biscuits from Tally, 'before they start fighting over that one.'

At almost two years old, Lili was a slightly built child with silky dark curls and big dark eyes. Tally had officially adopted her. The couple divided their time between London and their home in the South of France. In the latter's warmer climate, Lili's eczema had improved beyond all expectations. As she clutched her beaker the little girl rested against Tally's knee with one hand clutching at her skirt. Prone to being a little clingy, Lili was as deeply attached to her adoptive mother as Tally was to her. Shortly before Timon was born, Tally had read the letter that Oleia had left for Sander and she had cried over the sadness of it, knowing that, some day when Lili was old enough to understand adult relationships, she would give it to her daughter to read.

The two children were very different. Lili was highly strung and wary of anything or anybody new, but still a good deal calmer than she had been as a baby. Even at just over a year of age, Timon was her opposite in nature. He was naturally confident and unafraid and a real little rip, with his father's independent streak. Sometimes Tally felt she needed eyes in the back of her head to keep tabs on her lively son and she was grateful to have the support of a nanny to help her look after the children. Timon had learned to talk and walk early. His father's parents had pronounced him a handsome little boy but Tally was well aware that Sander's mother was still keen to have another granddaughter and thought that perhaps in a year or so she might consider having a third baby.

In the meantime two young children felt like plenty. Her pregnancy with Timon had proved an anxious time for her and Sander, because even with all the extra checks put in place to ensure a safe delivery both of them had secretly worried that something might go wrong. Sander had treated Tally like the finest and most breakable porcelain for the duration of her pregnancy and the unreserved joy with which they both welcomed Timon into the world was a fair testimony to the love they shared.

Crystal had got the job as a buyer for a string of boutiques and had recently been headhunted by a leading department store with a subsequent very welcome rise in salary. She loved working in the fashion world and adored the foreign travel and the shows, not to mention the discounted clothing she had access to. She was presently very excited about the prospect of buying her first apartment and had announced that she was 'off' men. Tally believed her mother was simply enjoying her independence.

Binkie, who had retired from her job in Devon, visited them regularly in London and her granddaughter was currently working as their nanny. In fact, the biggest change in Sander and Tally's family connections had taken place with Anatole, his wife, Ariadne, and daughter, Cosima. When Sander and Tally had attended Anatole's birthday party the year before, Tally had met all her father's relatives and new ties had been forged. Her father's wife had gone out of her way to give them a warm welcome. Tally had reaped the greatest pleasure from her new closeness with Cosima.

Her design firm had gone from strength to strength and Robert Miller had finally consented to allowing Sander to buy out his partnership. Robert was currently dating a very glamorous American model and, if the tabloids were to be believed, it was a serious relationship.

When their nanny had taken the children indoors for a bath, Sander closed a hand round Tally's wrist and tugged her down onto his spread thighs. He brushed teasing fingers through her marmalade-coloured corkscrew curls. 'Did anyone ever tell you that you have very sexy hair?'

'Someone might have done. That could be why I don't have it straightened any more,' she whispered, green eyes alight with amusement. 'Talk about weird tastes…'

Sander twisted her slim body round to find her mouth

and tasted her lush lips with unmistakeable hunger. 'Weird...' she teased again.

His fingertips glided up the taut skin of her inner thigh and her breath caught in her throat, desire drowning her sense of fun. '*Sander...*' she muttered in another tone entirely, her delicately rounded figure tut.

'I love you, Mrs Volakis, and very possibly I love you more every day I'm with you and the children. I didn't know having a family could feel so good.'

Her eyes sparkled with irrepressible humour. 'Then, as you once said, you're a slow learner!'

Dark golden eyes bright with appreciation of that quip and glinting in the sunshine, Sander sprang upright and carried her with him, pinning her to his lean, powerful length with possessive hands so that he could kiss her into breathless surrender. They clung to each other like magnets, their pleasure in one another intoxicating...

\* \* \* \* \*

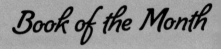

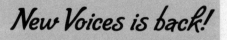